To Marine
for the first blue eyes
on the very first text

to Salomé
for her constant attention
in the middle of the night and across the Atlantic

to Alice D.
for the wisdom of her criticism
and her propensity to make me work
in unlikely places

. . . to Alexandre.

TAKE THIS MAN

Alice Zeniter

TAKE THIS MAN

*Translated from the French
by Alison Anderson*

Europa
editions

Europa Editions
214 West 29th Street
New York, N.Y. 10001
www.europaeditions.com
info@europaeditions.com

Translation by Alison Anderson
Original title: *Jusque dans nos bras*
Translation copyright © 2011 by Europa Editions

This work has been published thanks to the support from the
French Ministry of Culture – Centre National du Livre
Ouvrage publié avec le concours du
Ministère français chargé de la Culture – Centre National du Livre

Library of Congress Cataloging in Publication Data is available
ISBN 978-1-60945-053-3

Zeniter, Alice
Take This Man

Book design by Emanuele Ragnisco
www.mekkanografici.com
Cover photo © A J James/Getty Images

Prepress by Grafica Punto Print – Rome

Printed in Canada

TAKE THIS MAN

My generation will be worse off than my parents', my generation wasn't born with the internet but grew up with it and matured with it, and I have such a tender connection with the internet.

My generation is all about international terrorism and globalization, my generation doesn't dream about Hollywood but about London, Paris, Tokyo, and Singapore, my generation is all about traders who have to do without their twin towers.

My generation dreamt up Isla Moda, and the scientific solution to the perfectly natural requirement of having a swimming pool on board an Airbus, my generation repatriates people on charter planes, my generation is all about bling and Patek Philippe watches.

My generation lost the singer Bertrand Cantat and discovered Lithuania at the same time.

My generation is one of geeks and computer nerds who no longer have any use for manuscripts and have discovered e-books.

My generation is growing up with fake boobs and fake noses and hymen reconstruction surgery on demand, my generation is all about *Big Brother, Survivor, Secret Story,* and *The Weakest Link*.

My generation saw order restored after May '68, my generation tried to imitate May '68, my generation starts daydreaming as soon as May comes around, my generation doesn't have a clue where these classes that are supposed to be struggling might have gone to.

My generation speaks *franglais,* a mix of English and French, like in *Jeune & Jolie*: *la* story of the month *c'est quand* my girl hands her phone to a *keum sur le* dance floor *en mode* easy and he looks like *très* open, my generation watched Saddam Hussein get hanged on Dailymotion, my generation wins movie contests on cell phones and makes music with alpha waves.

My generation doesn't make babies anymore but doesn't automatically wear condoms either, but my generation was born with AIDS, my generation has never known safe sex, my generation fucks with rubber and a reconstructed hymen, my generation thinks there's no shame in meeting on Meetic, my generation thinks there's no shame in getting married on Meetic, my generation sells sex tapes on www.sextapes.com and hopes to earn the five thousand dollars the website promises, my generation drags itself in front of the courts hoping to make a profit on those videos.

My generation is forced to be green because of all those who never were, my generation is expected to go back to shitting in sawdust and stop taking baths, my generation thinks wind turbines are beautiful and they bury their houses underground, my generation won't have any oil left, just when we were starting to enjoy those low-cost flights.

My generation turned ten during the genocide in Rwanda.

My generation likes to buy mousepads.

My generation has visited every capital in Europe.

My generation's seen the end of sporting records, unless you resort to cryonics.

My generation is getting poorer, and will be paying for other people's retirement, and has learned to be afraid of old people, my generation has fewer and fewer civil servants, my generation believed in the Scandinavian model, my generation is ashamed to make mistakes in English because *it's not a foreign language for anyone anymore,* my generation has swung to the right because they despair of the view to the left, my generation has seen the welfare state dismantled before their eyes, my generation works more to earn more, my generation is poorly guided by guidance counselors, my generation has hedge funds and Jérôme Kerviel, my fucking generation is where you can lose five billion dollars walking out the door and pretending you didn't see a thing—Excuse me, did you happen to see five billion dollars anywhere? I must have dropped them on the way out the door. No? Are you sure?

My generation witnesses pedophile trials and knows the truth that no longer comes from the mouth of babes.

My generation is the Posh and Becks generation, along with anorexia, and paparazzi, and stars who walk around without their underwear and don't fasten their kids' seatbelts, my generation has seen sperm stains on the dresses of interns who solemnly swear to America.

My generation is all about first ladies who make record albums, it's the Eurodisney generation.

My generation is all about no-smoking laws and Red Bull and vodka.

My generation is all into iPods and iPhones and USB keys and Wifi and MSN, my generation friends on Facebook, my generation pokes.

My generation is going sterile trying to have kids at forty.

My generation has rediscovered poker and might discover all the intrinsic properties of black matter and isn't the least bit impressed by travel to the moon.

My generation hasn't yet handed down its verdict: is Paris Hilton a hottie or not?

My generation is the subprime mortgage crisis generation.

My generation has global warming and tearful documentaries about polar bears and melting icecaps.

My generation can no longer deal with all the poverty in the world but it should be the other way around and what else oh yeah my generation rides scooters and steals scooters and pays

for DNA tests to find their stolen scooters, and in my generation there are seventeen million people in France who read the
tabloids, and above all my generation is constantly being told
that our lives will be worse and not better, my generation is all
about unemployment and real estate bubbles and camps for
illegal immigrants and Showcase television and rich people
becoming citizens of Monaco and capital flight and tax havens
and the elimination of the 35-hour work week and transport
credits and computerized police surveillance where you can't
even make a phone call if they suspect you are a member of an
organized gang, or belong to a generation where there's no
order, a generation that lost Kurt Cobain but who are told
repeatedly that they can win the war for purchasing power.

It comes to me all of a sudden, as I reach the steps of the *mairie,* the list is there in my head, flashing and burning inside, and it almost makes me want to throw up. I wonder if I'm right to go through with this. I look at Mad on my left and he gives me a tense smile and I wonder if it isn't a really dumbass thing we're doing, and it's getting me so psyched that I think maybe all the defects of my generation ought to just *die out* with us, and we shouldn't have anything to do with other people, maybe there's no point in helping each other and we should just find ourselves our own little bunkers and lock ourselves up in there while we wait for the world or our generation to go extinct, because there's too much crap going on inside, outside, everywhere.

But Mad is there on my left and in spite of my nails digging ever deeper into his arm, through the cloth of the suit he bought just for the occasion—a dead cheap suit but he looks handsome in it, and stoic—he isn't wondering *what are we waiting for to set everything on fire*, he's waving to the Arabesque who's walking behind us and I breathe more deeply.

And I say to myself, over and over, *I do yes I do*, I will say yes I do. Not like some princess, not as if it were the most beautiful day of my life, not as if I was swimming in swirls of organdy with fake flowers that are finely veined on their petals, not as if there were some huge white wedding cake with the little plastic couple on top—remember, you laughed about that with Mad, he said he didn't even think you could find a little plastic couple with a black groom and a white bride, or maybe only among the supplies of some post-apartheid educational system—and it wasn't like my mother was weeping for joy, or we were about to go on some honeymoon, or that someone would take a photograph of the entire family, and there wouldn't be any reception either, just *I do yes I do*, I do.

Behind us I hear the Arabesque telling Jérémie to hold her bag and she pulls out a little disposable camera and she snaps away at Mad and me with a laugh. And she says, One more, one more, and I'm looking past the lens at the people waiting for the 38 bus on the traffic island in the middle of the avenue. There's a fat woman draped in madras, and an old guy bent almost double, and two little black girls with pigtails braided with bright bright pink. They look at me, too, and I can tell they're disappointed by my outfit.

The Arabesque had warned me that it was "just really drab, Alice . . . " She wanted to try on all the bridesmaid's gowns in the cheap stores before the wedding, she tried on tempests of raw silk and lace, with roses on the bodice and skirts split up the side, and a matching headband with a little dove.

The Arabesque acted more like a bride than I did—she's the one who took pleasure in cutting things out of catalogues and in seeing my expression in the multi-matrimonial boutique when I said, No, something simple, just simple, to the sales-woman who cooed and wore a brooch in the shape of a frog with red eyes.

Then the Arabesque suggested, What about a boubou? Wouldn't you like to get married in a boubou? It would show your love for Mad's culture, and naturally she drawled as she said the word love and waited for me to react and I said, Yeah, sure, and why don't I pound millet with my toes while I'm at it, and the frog woman said, I beg your pardon? and I mumbled, Mind your own business. But the Arabesque had her hypocritical smile on like when she's in a really good mood and she said, Her fiancé is from Mali. I know she said it hoping the woman would get all flustered or afraid and that way the Arabesque could get a kick out of seeing her pathetic racism, but the saleswoman simply said, Oh, I see, but you know everyone does like this style so unless you want a boubou I would recommend this style, it really suits you, particularly around the waist, hmm, don't you think it emphasizes it nicely?

Hmm, I was thinking I'd be getting married in my beige hundred percent cotton dress from H&M, and I'd known it all along, and it made me sad to see the saleswoman who looked like she really believed in what she did, she believed in that style, inspired by a frivolous shepherdess, and she believed in my future happiness and all the bullshit the mayor would be feeding us about love and helping one another and the beauty of commitment. So I concentrated on the frog and I didn't say anything, while the Arabesque mulled over her disappointment.

The Arabesque is really the witness to our marriage, not just to the ceremony that is waiting for us as soon as we go through the door (and you're trying not to think about it as you look at the pediment because you know that otherwise you'll be so scared you'll turn around) but also to the Years that Went Before, the years of the Great History of Racism that has led to this, and the whole investigative procedure, and all the questionnaires. The Arabesque could be charged with perjury, she has sworn that I love Mad, she has sworn that Mad loves me, she has sworn you cannot find anything more romantic than this marriage between two childhood friends who have discovered at last that they are made for each other, and now that she's at the foot of the steps she is shoving me to get me to walk forward, and she can't stop laughing.

You suppose it's funny. The fact you're holding him close, this guy you've done so much with: made your first painting— Starry Night, half gouache, half pasta shells—and held your first masquerade contest, and smoked your first cigarette, your first joint, and started your first ephemeral music band, and even voted—the first time it was about whether France should belong to Europe and Mad was there next to you in the booth going eeny meeny miney mo over the ballot, and before his first night with his girlfriend you told him all about how a woman's body works,·drawing diagrams on a Kleenex, and he was the guy who wore your bra over his shoulder to drive your friends crazy, and he swore you didn't know how to go about getting a guy and keeping him, it was practically pathological, and now your best friend, best buddy, blood brother, your *bro* standing there in his gray pin-striped suit is about to become your husband, any minute now, because why? Because of this famous Great History of Racism that you and he and the Arabesque have traced back to its roots, so many times, and by virtue of the powers invested in you by your nationality—the power of transmission, the power to turn him into a French citizen by the grace of a wedding band.

As I climb the steps, counting them, no matter how frightened I am, my heart practically pounding against my teeth, I know I cannot *not* go through with it, simply because Mad and I, ever since I was three years old, we've been sharing almost everything, and he's the kid who shared half his comforter with me when we went on our first school ski trip and I'd forgotten mine: well, that kid deserves a piece of my nationality too if he wants it.

But you still don't really know, as you go into the lobby and the cool air surrounds you and dries the sweat on your skin that smells of fear while Mad is asking for the reception, you still don't really know how you ended up here about to get married, at this *mariage blanc* where there's no white dress. Because you remember the day when Mad asked you to marry him and it was so strange that . . . but the problem, really, is how did he come to be so sure you'd say *I do yes I do*, I do, for better and for worse until death do us part?

So while you can see the deputy mayor at the far side of the room and he's smiling and beckoning you toward him with great sweeps of his arms, and you can hear your sisters scraping the legs of their chairs over the tile floor as they sit down in the front row, you're really thinking it's a pity you don't exactly know what the hell you're doing in the *mairie* of the tenth arrondissement. Because in a few minutes they're going to ask you, and you cannot afford to hesitate.

It was because of the square sand box in the kindergarten playground. My older sister claimed she'd found a dead bird when she was digging, and after that I never wanted to go back there to play. It started with the plump little blond girl who had freckles everywhere, like all over, right down to her fingernails, because she was the first one, while she was adjusting her multi-colored butterfly eyeglasses, those big thick eyeglasses that make a kid's face look just too small, she was the first one who started on the endless cycle of the word *bougnoule*, yes, right there in the sandbox between what was left of a hotel complex that probably had carriages with white horses, and the plastic shovel the school had lent us, with its broken handle that had been taped together, because more than once you tried to dig a hole to the center of the earth to see THE ball of fire that Mommydaddy told you was in the middle.

So I don't know, maybe she wanted the shovel and obviously I wanted to finish the west wing of my hotel and we had to agree who would be the queen at the first ball, the one we'd throw when we opened the big hotel complex. And sure, I was the one who was determined to be queen since it was my idea in the first place, and I was the one who'd designed the plans and built it and named all the horses, too, and who had the shovel in her hand to begin with, anyway, it was me, it was always me.

I wasn't trying to be selfish but there was only one Ken in

my whole pile of Barbies that I brought every morning to show how all our sandbox hotel complexes were coming along, how there was a giant solid gold bathroom on the right, and on the left a four poster bed as big as a soccer pitch with secret passages leading to their other friends' bedrooms and to the dressing room, which naturally was gigantic to accommodate all their farthingales and crinolines.

There could only be one queen of the ball, and the other one was doomed to go home at midnight in her special carriage on the orders of her strict and formidable father—which is when my cousin stopped playing Action Man and he gave me this wizard, who entered the scene, *the greatest of all heroes*, and he could frown and move his arms. All the Barbies were afraid of him, even the punkette—my sister had chopped her hair off and painted her mouth black—and they all obeyed whenever he moved his arms up and down with a squawk of mechanical laughter.

When you're that age you never wonder why the blonds are always the good guys and the dark-haired ones are always the bad guys, as if it were perfectly normal for Goldilocks and Lady Lovely Locks and Candy and Sleeping Beauty and Grace Kelly to inspire trust, as if their white skin and gold hair were pledges of good faith. But the bad guys were like the wizard and they had dark hair and dark skin and their names were Jet like the one in your morning cartoon. Because it made sense that way, they could hide in the shadow and eavesdrop on conversations and hatch up terrible plots during the night, so yeah, the dark-haired ones were the bad guys and the wizard couldn't play Barbie's understanding father because he still had his black hair and black beard and that little grimace on his face that meant none of you could trust him; even when he tried to be kind there was always someone who said, Girls, there's something fishy going on here. Like in *Robin Hood.*

But the wizard wasn't the Barbies' most terrifying enemy;

he was no match for the Pulcinella rag doll that I'd had ever since I was little and I'd always thought this doll had the most terrifying, absolutely perverse smile. A smile so terrible that when Pulcinella joined in the game it was always so he could do a really good job of attacking the Barbies, tearing off all their clothes, breaking their arms, raping them and then hanging them upside down from the treadwheel crane, he was so awful that we always teamed up to defeat him by making him ingurgitate sleeping medicine made from chalk powder and blades of grass and mud, and when he fell asleep we'd jump on him and quickly-quickly we'd lock him up in the pocket of my schoolbag so he could never ever get out again.

Naturally, Pulcinella only attacked the most beautiful, sparkling Barbie, the queen of the ball, the one whose fall would be the most spectacular and who would make the most thrilling slave. This title I aimed for whenever I played with my friends was not without its share of dangers, and I knew it, because outside the hotel, where the guards with their earflaps could no longer keep an eye on my magnificence, Pulcinella, a smile on his face, was waiting for me to go right by him so he could grab me . . .

Pulcinella wasn't dark-haired. But you have to figure that if you spent your life with a multi-colored bonnet on your head it might be even worse than having black hair. Pulcinella was a hundred times more marginal than the wizard. And a hundred times scarier. Who would ever trust a guy who never takes off his bonnet with a bell on it? None of your Barbies, for a start.

That day in the sandbox there was the usual squabble over who got to do what. I had my Snow White Barbie in my right hand, and the shovel in the left, and my freckled friend was dressing the Nightingale princess that she had managed to nick from me just when I was taking the dolls out of my schoolbag, which was really unfair because the Nightingale princess had everything it took to be queen of the ball and so she was MY doll, in principle, with her turquoise dress and crown of flowers. I started negotiating to have at least the nightingale—or was it the Bluebird?—hoping he'd be enough for Snow White to win the title and marry Ken in the huge salon of the hotel complex and then—

And then she said *dirty bougnoule*, just dirty *bougnoule*. Around the sandbox were the usual friends listening to the usual arguments and everyone laughed, including me, because it's a funny word—and even now when you think of it, trying not to add skinhead or Doc Martens to the picture, it really is a silly word with a funny sound—so off they went, *bougnoule* ha ha ha. I reached out to pick up the nightingale and conclude the bargain and then I asked her to say it again so I wouldn't forget it before I went home, that new word, a new insult that my sister wouldn't know, for sure, and I was looking forward to really lording it over her. What's that you said? And it made me laugh a second time, made me think of a big fat face, like a Buddha chewing on his dinner, a face with something like buttocks. But since I had to get back at my girlfriend somehow, I told her she looked like she got her suntan through a sieve because of her freckles, and we all laughed and shouted, Eat some sand, not even thinking there could be any link between *bougnoule* and dark skin, and then—

I was in the living room at home, behind the sagging leather sofa that the cats had all scratched up, between the sofa and the piano that Mommydaddy bought because all three of us girls played the piano and we swore, cross my heart and hope to die, that we'd go on playing long enough to make it worth it. Between the sofa and the piano we were fighting with my sister over a little wooden bicycle and I could tell the time had come when the argument would really get out of hand and I'd been waiting for just that moment ever since I got home so I'd be able to use my new sandbox word, the word I was so proud of. So off we went with an avalanche of insults that were pretty basic to begin with, like rotten potato or stinkbottom and then we added a few wild animals like you're as ugly as a hippopotamus's ass, and then a fat hippopotamus and I can't remember the last thing my sister said because the time had come for me to trumpet triumphantly and real loud—I wanted Mommydaddy to hear too how I had enriched my vocabulary:

DIRTY BOUGNOULE

And I knew right away something was wrong. Because Mommydaddy stood up: What did you say just now, repeat what you just said? You could see from the look in their eyes that they weren't asking the question because they were surprised I had such a good grasp of the language, no, it looked like they were filled with a kind of anger I'd hardly ever seen on their faces, a sad sort of anger, the kind that made you feel horribly guilty, a sad anger that was the most lethal of all Mommydaddy's weapons.

I said "*bougnoule*," removing the *dirty* in hopes that it might make it seem not quite so bad. Because I already knew that *dirty* was enough to turn any word into an insult, even the most inoffensive ones like when you said *dirty cat* to the cat who was pissing us off begging for his food or jumping on the expensive piano, the cross my heart hope to die piano that was bought for the three daughters.

Do you know what it means, *bougnoule*? I didn't know, or course I didn't know. And who are you talking to? I don't know, Daddy. Well, don't ever say it again.

It wasn't that you wanted to hurt Mommydaddy, on the contrary, you were ready to forget that new word that seemed so funny at the time, that was such a big hit at the sandbox and had even meant your friend won the title of queen of the ball. You agreed never to use it again but just then you couldn't: you needed to know what it was, where it was located on the scale of words-you-must-never-use-ever-again, the words that included bitch, which you used on your sister during a slide-across-the-floor-in-the-kitchen contest, *bitch* and it had earned you a major spanking and after that it was the referent of all words-you-must-never-use-ever-again. At the stage of linguistic development you were at, it was simply unthinkable to let *bougnoule* go by without getting an explanation from Mommydaddy.

So I went and looked all sad, put on my official cute face that nine times out of ten would get me off the spanking, that much I knew from years of experience, and I went on asking but why but why?

Mommydaddy sighed, and dampened down their sad anger a little and then they said, Look, Alice, it is a very mean expression to talk about people like your dad who come from another country outside of France and in particular a country in North Africa or the Middle East, but it really is very mean and nasty, you know, Punkin, it's really *racist.*

What were you supposed to know about racism when you were only four or five years old and you still had a plump belly like some village notable, and your hair only grew at the back of your skull which made you look not like a little girl but like a dwarf, a very old dwarf, so that when long after that you saw the first pictures of Jedi Master Yoda you immediately felt a sort of bond with him, thinking back on the photo album of your early life . . .

How much did you understand at the time? For years it was really very vague, and even if you had grasped that it was some sort of absolute evil, even if you remembered Mommydaddy's sad anger and how it ignited a flare of intense hatred in you whenever you heard the word "racist," you still had to admit you found it very hard to identify the enemy among the people around you. This wasn't entirely your fault. What were you supposed to do when you were faced with a sort of racism that was as joyful as the one in your sandbox?

When I was in elementary school my best friend among the boys was Amadou—he hadn't started using his monosyllabic nickname yet, which almost made me forget he had a real first name—and he was from Mali. The other children used to shout at him, "They washed you inside a chicken!" For a long time I wondered why and I still didn't understand. But that meaningless phrase, that sort of came out of nowhere, at the time it felt a lot more obviously racist than "*bougnoule.*" *They washed you inside a chicken*—why, somebody tell me?—was a terrible insult and Amadou got really pissed every time, and I did too, and that was when the pebble fights, which have since gone down in schoolyard history, began.

There were two sides, like in any fight. But there wasn't really any ideology behind the pebble throwing, so from one day to the next there were any number of renegades, and I never forgave Laura for having abandoned the left flank of my army on the pretext that I had stolen some pogs from her coat pocket. Which wasn't true at all. I had simply reclaimed the pogs she had won by cheating and which by right were mine. From one end of the soccer pitch to the other the two sides were throwing gravel along with the foam balls that were used for dodgeball but which never hurt as much as we would have liked. My sister made a slingshot and the elastic always came undone just before you shot the stone but in theory it represented a major advance in our arms race.

One day a girl in our army stumbled over a foam ball and fell down on the soccer pitch and broke her teeth. The teacher found out just how serious our pitched battles had become, dividing the schoolyard, and we were all summoned to the covered part of the yard where the principal started to tell us off. He seemed really surprised to learn that what had started our war was the accusation of *getting washed inside a chicken.* He didn't grasp the racist connotation, he didn't realize that behind the absurdity of the expression Amadou and I knew that it referred to the dirt of black skin and Barbarian customs of evisceration—how else were you supposed to get washed *inside* a chicken if you didn't cut it open, plain and simple? The principal gave some wishy-washy lecture about respect and the dangers of foam balls that might look harmless, but no one was listening to his speech: we were all too busy kicking each other in the ankles and murmuring "War, war!" and my sister was hiding behind her friend Alexandra's pink raincoat repairing her slingshot, and we swore we would never give up our struggle for freedom.

But in reality we were all capable of being racists one day and blacks the next, and the war didn't last for very long.

Groups formed and disbanded, and the color of your skin or your sweater—anything could lead to a new alliance, although this system of alliances never ever managed to destroy my friendship with Amadou, and I'd already planned out my life with him: I'd buy a circus where I'd be the circus rider, not because I loved horses but for the sequined leotard, and he'd be the lion tamer-magician-trumpeter; we'd adopt a dozen kids who'd become acrobats and violinists; I'd have plastic surgery to give myself the green eyes I dreamt of; we'd invent a vaccine against AIDS—something you suspect your cat died of, at least according to the vet—which would make us millions and billions of dollars, or more precisely however much money it would take to fulfill our greatest ambition: to buy the château of Versailles.

We stuck to our program for a long time, even after the games around us had changed and made us forget the first racist sentence of our life. "They washed you inside a chicken" disappeared when everyone started playing *lice*, throwing imaginary lice at each other and protecting themselves by brandishing the unbreakable anti-lice mirror. We all started insulting any kid who had long thick hair, like that slut Julie who went around nonchalantly shaking her mane, while

Amadou had to be sure he didn't get washed inside a chicken, and all the boys in the class always gave Julie their Kinder Egg toys because—she's the one who came out and said it but everyone was absolutely convinced of it anyway—she looked like the little girl in the ad for Kinder Eggs on television, the one who says, But of course, Michel, I always have Kinder chocolate at home.

In elementary school we could be just as racist against blonds, in fact the majority of us were, not like some little minority who were tired of being persecuted and decided to hate the majority of those who were persecuting them, no, the dark-haired whites and the dark-haired *bougnoules* and the dark-haired inside-a-chicken bathers would all gang up against the blonds and shout at them that they had lice, gigantic huge lice with fifty thousand little legs that were eating away at their scalps and were going to drink all their blood and you could see the lice all the way from the back of the classroom and on the far side of the schoolyard they had gotten that fat from drinking their brains and so on until that slut Julie went off to cry behind the fir tree and the dark-haired kids were declared the victors of the lice war.

On February 22, 2008, Mad came to my little student apartment in the tenth arrondissement. There's a white church on this street, and flowers on all the balconies, and a squeaky hardwood floor and across the landing behind the dark red door there's a neighbor who has who hated me ever since I had my housewarming party, when Dahlia puked all over her doormat.

He had just spent the day at the Préfecture to renew his residence permit and, as usual, it made him hopping mad, and he was smoking one cigarette after the other, and when he got to the end of the pack he methodically crumpled it up in his fist and folded the cellophane film that was around it into little squares, smaller and smaller, until it made a tiny little ball in his fingers.

He played with it for a few minutes before tossing it into my fish-shaped ashtray and then he melted it with his lighter. When he had used up all the potential activities offered by a pack of cigarettes he looked up and said, I can't take it any more, Alice, the way they all look, the glasses they wear, and their noses when the glasses slide down, and the way they cough, and that faint smile of theirs when I stutter or mix up my words even though, fuck, I don't make any mistakes in French, *at all*, I've been speaking their shit language from the day I was born, I speak pure French, I've even read everything, I grew up with all those books they'll never read, with their fat noses and slimy hands and the little slurping noises they make when they suck on their lower lip and make that constipated face, and you know damn well when I want I can speak French as elegantly as anyone on the planet.

I listened to Mad without speaking, because this wasn't the first time this had happened. Ever since the last time he came back to France, all grown up, his own master, he has had to go to the Préfecture every year with his work contract and letters of recommendation from his employer, and his electricity bills, and his report cards from French high school, all in order to avoid the mortal insult of being told he has to take the DILF[1]. When the 2006 law was passed obliging foreigners to prove their level of French, Mad began to tremble at the thought of that test. He wasn't afraid of failing, on the contrary, Mad was just *too* good in French, and you remembered how at the lycée he had his Mallarmé period when he spoke in virtually nothing but quotations from *Grands faits divers* and *Coup de dés* and how angry he would make you when he said everything was "depth of basalt and lava." So of course a person like Mad, with his exquisite corpses and convoluted expressions, who was always ready to compete with you to see who'd be first to finish reading a particular book, found it unspeakably humiliating to have to prove to them that he knew how to read the time in some TV magazine and look up which channel a particular program was going to be on, like, if he came home from work at six fifteen in the evening, which programs could he watch?

For three years now Mad had been juggling with all sorts of incomprehensible acronyms: CST, CESEDA, L-311[2] . . . And you're the sort who never even knows which box to tick for your housing benefits, so you looked at him aghast as he filled

[1] "Diplôme initial de langue française" – a sort of TOEFL exam. (T.N.)
[2] Temporary residence card; code governing the admission of foreigners and rights to asylum; article in the CESEDA concerning the "provisions relative to residency documents." (T.N.)

out forms that were completely hermetic as far as you were concerned, and sometimes as you were leaning over his shoulder you read stuff that was as terrifying as, "According to the JO of July 25, 2006, there is no VLS required to obtain a CST VPF." So you were used to Mad getting angry. You knew he had to calm down before he could talk about it with you, and that to calm down he first had to let out a stream of words all in a jumble, sometimes completely meaningless, but quickly and spasmodically, Mad spitting out his words like bullets from a machine gun, until he was wheezing, until he had to lean forward to try and catch his breath, as if it were just there in front of him, in the air, in the room, he would lean forward and grab it then on he went.

I'm fed up, Alice, fed up, sometimes I'd like to kill them, tear them limb from limb like some garland of paper cut-outs, and turn them and their files into tiny bits of confetti to fly around the room, I want to slam my fists on their Plexiglas window, and I know, oh don't I know, that they'd like nothing better—then they could release their dogs and have them tear at my calves until the blood and flesh show red beneath my black skin. But when they tell me I don't have all my papers, papers that don't even exist, Alice, it's like someone asking you when you show up at university, Where's your fairy dust? This just won't do! Except that we're all trembling because we're too frightened to think, we might actually believe this paper really exists, so we go home and look for it everywhere, feverishly, in those enormous files we keep just in case, for the Préfecture, for the interview they finally condescend to grant you, shoving their glasses up their sweaty noses, so we start calling around to try and find that fairy dust, we call the French administrative offices but they're in on the joke and they're not about to help us, ever, they just laugh discreetly into their telephone receivers and leave us to worry about it.

So if you leave the Préfecture at that point, and you believe them, and you go to hunt for that document, then you're fucked, screwed, for good, it's the rule that will eliminate you, because it means they'll have fewer cases to deal with. So the thing is you have to stay there no matter what, even if the roof caves in, even if the phone on the wall rings until you pick up and they tell you your family has been kidnapped, even if they pay actors to come in and scream that World War III has just started and you have to go down into the bomb shelter, even if you can smell something burning and they tell you it's your own house that's on fire, and maybe your little sister is trapped in there, you stay, and you don't move, you stay and stay and you can stay silent if you want to, in any case they won't ever listen to you as if you were an actual human being, they have their eye on you, they're just waiting for you to forget to use a definite article, or mix up your genders, or say "tou" instead of "tu," but they couldn't care less whether what you say makes any sense.

They just laughed at me when I said I had a job, and the only thing I could show them was that stupid contract for the shoe store, because after my father died, you know, it was hard for me to go back to my studies after two years back in Mali, and now they are laughing at me because I want a student card, because at last I can—how do they put it—justify my enrolment in a French institute of higher education. And just now this fat woman behind the plastic cage at the counter said to me, What a good idea, to want to study, but you know she's really thinking, What will they think of next to try and fuck us around to stay here? So you know what, with this fucking student card, I might get a longer residence permit but no right to Social Security! The drain on their funds—don't look at me! Their fairy tale about the polygamous black man getting thousands of euros in child support, that's not me either! You know what I am, for them? I'm peanuts, girl. The worst of it is that it's all connected, everything. You know that if I had a Diploma of Higher Education I could already have filed my request for naturalization? It reduces the number of years of residence in France required before you can submit your application. But how can I go back to my studies if I have to prove I can support myself in order to get a card which, in any case, will restrict the amount of hours I'm allowed to work?

So then the woman said, But what is it you want, Monsieur, a student permit or a work permit? Because if you don't know, I can't know for you, and besides in half an hour I have to close, and I swear that every minute or so she would discreetly pinch her nostrils as if I smelled bad, and after a while she'd almost convinced me that I did. I just wanted to go home and take a shower, and rub off the smell of death, scrape at my skin until it bled, until it smelled of bleach. I wish you could have seen her, seen the whole lot of them. They are so no finer than us, their bodies like drooping noisily behind their desks, with their photos of their kids and Post-its all over their computer screens, and their doodles of stars and little stick figures. I swear there are times I practically hallucinate and I'm sure they're going to start drawing swastikas. I almost feel like telling them, go ahead, it's hardly going to make any difference at this point. I've seen your shit laws closing round my neck, more and more, Sarko's in 2006 and Hortefeux's in 2007—what better way to tell me how much you hate me?[3]

And they creak, yes, that's what it is, their joints creak, their mouths hiss, their noses whistle, and the papers crackle beneath their fingers, and stick to their fingers, and the paper clips rattle on the desk, and then eventually they tell you it's okay, you win, you've worn them down, but do you really want to go on all your life having to renew that permit, huh? And you know what it all means, behind all the laws and words? It means, go home, nigra, so I can get home a little earlier tonight.

[3] An anti-terror law authorizing increased government surveillance of the population; a law tightening immigration. (T.N.)

They are lying when they say *love it or leave it*, you know, Alice, because they'll never let us love it. The minute you say you love France, right away they give you a funny look, and they start staring at you and at your hands as if they're going to find traces of something chemical, some powder, explosives, bombs, because it's bound to be a lie, you're just saying that so you can stay, and integrate. Sure, I get the impression I'm insinuating myself with people, that's the impression they give me, like water among stones, I feel like that whenever I take the métro, I can't walk normally anymore. Truth is, you have the choice of leaving the country or leaving the country. The only difference is when. They're just there to tell you it's *temporary*, got it, nigra, you no go mess with my country. But you know the worst of it is that because of them I've started thinking this time it's too much, this time it's as if they were exploding my head with the way they look at me, with all that pressure they put on me, and I told myself: They're right, they're fucking right, I don't want to be doing this all my life, renewing my papers and then seeing them again, I don't have the courage, to see her again, that woman who looks like some baby mouse when they're still all pink and blind and practically shapeless, know what I mean, so *No way*, I thought to myself, *No way*, I can't go on like this, I can't take it any more.

Mad paused to catch his breath. His left hand was nervously twisting the edge of my Ikea carpet, just the spot where there were already all those cigarette burns. I asked him, So what does this mean, will you go back to Mali to live?

No, Alice, I want to get French nationality. Whatever it takes.

In middle school racism was already more clear-cut. When Amadou went to Mali he promised to bring me a super-huge djembe because I was fed up with the piano and I wanted to be a percussionist, but big-time, so a gigantic djembe. You mean as big as the table? I mean the biggest drum that ever existed. Alice, even the customs officials at the airport will say, Excuse me, sir, but I'm not sure that drum will fit in the baggage hold, and I'll say, Look guys, please make an effort because I promised a friend in France that I'd bring her this drum, so do your best. And do you think they'll obey? Of course they'll obey, mademoiselle, what choice do they have, they are going to be absolutely floored by your impressive drum . . .

Amadou's departure made me think about my own rapport with Africa. He was born in Mali, then came and spent a few years in France, and now he was going home again. He's the one who'd said it, *A drum from home*. And for years I'd been listening to my own aunts saying "back in the *bled*" referring to their village and I was beginning to wonder where it was and what it must look like and how much I ought to think of it as home, too, since the countryside of Normandy suddenly seemed way too insipid and way too close. The few photographs that Mommydaddy had taken on one of their trips and which I'd gotten my hands on were totally satisfying in the exotic department: plenty of sand everywhere and there was even a donkey and a well. And a bit of arid mountain looming fiercely in one corner of the picture. So I decided then and there to change my notion of home. The next morning I started saying "back in the *bled*," thinking above all about the donkey. It would be ideal for going for rides in the mountain, besides, I think I'd never really recovered from my attachment to Cadichon, which Mommydaddy had made me read about in the stories of the Comtesse de Ségur, like every good little girl should.

So I embarked on a major endeavor to *algericize* myself. First of all, I discovered that the birthmark on my stomach was shaped like Africa. I was incredibly happy to find at last some physical particularity that seemed to emphasize my ties with Algeria, and when Mommydaddy made fun of my theory and asked me if I thought that the French all had maps of France or Michelin guides printed on their stomachs, I didn't answer and I didn't even think about their question.

Because apart from that Africa-shaped spot, I honestly don't look the least bit like an Arab, and in a way I'd like to take Mommydaddy with me wherever I go just so they can show people their dark skin and curly hair, and so what if Mommydaddy is half Norman, too, the other half provides ample proof of all the exoticism required.

Other than the birthmark there's nothing except, maybe, my lips. Well, and even then I'm not sure, because when I look in the mirror my lips tells me a lot less about jebels and the desert than the birthmark does. On the other hand, one day someone asked me—fuck, people ask me all the time—whether my last name was Alsatian, and when I answered, with a smile, the trumpets of Jericho in my voice, that *No*, my name was *Arabic,* the chick looked at me from head to foot and said, Oh, that's why you have big lips.

I told my family at dinner that night and my sister said, what's the big deal, it's true, you do have big lips, and even a big nose and big round cow's eyes, if you really want to know, but Mommydaddy said, Stop right there, and added, Some people are so prejudiced, I swear to God, and Mommydaddy murmured, Racist bitch. To be added to the list of words-you-mustn't-ever-say.

I was almost pleased to have these big Arab lips, even if when I read my comics or I looked at the powdered chocolate packet I realized the chick must have confused me with Black Africans—did Amadou have big lips? He'd left such a long time ago that I couldn't remember. Because the stereotypical Arab doesn't have big lips, it's more like little slit-eyes, a stupid hat shaped like a—shaped like nothing—and a carpet. But I was pleased all the same.

I was beginning to have an identity crisis, because of my need to feel Algerian, and the only words of Arabic I knew were the ones that I could use to ask my grandmother for cookies or make her smile. I felt these tremendous rushes of love for my grandmother, because she represented my entire *Algéritude*. My little corner of Algeria, braiding her long orange hair—at high school you started dying your hair with henna too, even though you got these big orange splashes staining your clothes the minute it started raining or you began to sweat, you didn't care, henna was a part of you, you were a part of henna, have you seen my birthmark?—and making her gold bracelets clink around her chubby wrists, and even after forty years in France, can you believe, she still could not say Marguerite so she ended up calling my mother Frigid or Fridge, she was that bad at pronouncing her name and whenever I cut my hair she moaned and she said I was too thin.

My grandmother always had a horde of aunts between the ages of twenty and fifty in her wake, and they would talk about husbands and ask me about my boyfriends, were they good-looking, and rich, and a few years later they snuck me cigarettes by the window in the kitchen and asked me whether my boyfriends were good lovers, and my grandmother and aunts would natter away in Arabic while Mommydaddy listened with a smile, with the vaguely condescending solicitude of the older brother, and then they'd interrupt to calm the aunts down whenever they got worked up about those no-good neighbors of theirs who were always borrowing dishes but didn't invite the family to Kader's wedding, or did invite them, but then my aunts took a dim view of marriage between Algerians and Moroccans because there were some major cultural differences that could get in the way of good mutual understanding.

When I asked Mommydaddy why my aunts thought that Moroccans were not like us they laughed when I said "us" and asked me what I meant by "us," well us Algerians, shit, haven't you seen my fabulous birthmark shaped like Africa? And then they said, Well it's probably because of the age-old saying whereby Algerians are warriors, Moroccans are shepherds, and Tunisians are women. A saying you can re-interpret any way you like depending on the country you come from, to insult your neighbors any way you liked, but as far as I was concerned, back in the days when I was in high school, I believed that saying, I was proud of it, the distant shores of Algeria seemed to be radiate with light from those words, and I was the girl in the TV ad for Algeria, wearing a keffiyeh and climbing the mountains of Great Kabylia, and turning to the camera to say that Algerians were warriors, Moroccans were shepherds and—I was really sorry for their sake, sudden wink to the television viewers—Tunisians were women.

At middle school I felt Algerian, I had the mark of Africa at the top of my stomach, and I wrote down words in Arabic in a little notebook and got my father to say them for me. It worked out well at high school because my two best friends were fantasizing about the guys from the urban development zone just over the way and I was a cultural alibi for them, their Arab friend, I showed them my notebook, we said "wallah" at the end of our sentences and "zarma" in the middle because we weren't really sure what it meant. When we went to rap concerts and the singers asked whether there was anyone there from Africa, my girlfriends would shout as loud as me. I taught them how to ululate, how to stick your tongue up against your palate, and I told them that was the Algerian way, because the other countries went no further than moving their lips and sticking their hand in front of their mouth to make it a sound box.

In middle school my favorite outfit was: beige flares, a black bustier and, of course, the green and black Sergio Tacchini jacket that Coralie was always lending me. I felt unstoppable in that outfit, and when Coralie and Aude and I got together, we'd swap our latest Lacoste perfume and gloss and black eye pencil and we'd smear it everywhere, clumsily—you can just see the wavy lines you made on your Pharaonic eyes with that heavy pencil—before we would go out and walk down the street, just for the sake of walking and to hang around or sometimes just practice walking the way you're supposed to. When we saw police cars we'd look down, quickly, so they wouldn't recognize us, because we were convinced that all the cops in the neighborhood were looking for us, and we'd whisper, fuck the cops, fuck the security agents, and we planned to write "faggots" on their car, but then we weren't sure how to spell it, one "g" or two, and then Aude suggested we could write FAG because that was easy, there were only three letters. Then we wondered if they stood for something, those three letters. It was only six years later that you saw the whole word properly spelled in a poem and you understood at last what it meant, and that FAG didn't stand for anything, either.

To jazz up my way cool look even more, I had a pair of really high platform shoes with really wide soles, like the ones the Spice Girls wore on one of the posters in my room, just no American flag on them, and I loved referring to them in Eng-

lish, "my platform shoes," even if the way they looked made
Mommydaddy laugh, and they were always offering to stick
them on the scale to check whether they weighed a ton or not.
Their sarcasm didn't faze me one bit because every time I said
"platform shoes" I got the impression I had oil drums on my
feet and that I belonged to OPEC and in those days at middle
school you weren't about to go carrying slogans around in your
head like the ones you'd be shouting later on, No Blood for
Oil, it was just a synonym of wealth, of being stinking rich, and
you could bet your life that some day soon you'd be buying
your own Sergio Tacchini jacket because Coralie deliberately
reminded you without fail whenever anyone complimented
you on your way cool look that it was her jacket. So you didn't
trust her, not really, even when you made her promise she
wouldn't, you didn't trust her because she might come out and
tell everyone, like in front of the boys on their mopeds, she
might even—and that would be the ultimate *shouma*—tell
Emilio Rodriguez, the handsomest one of all.

Obviously that wasn't his real name but we wanted to name
him after that sexy guy who was in that useless film about bad
neighborhoods with Michelle Pfeiffer who was trying to make
people believe she'd been in the Marines and that she could
kill a man with her bare hands, and Coralie said, If she can do
that, guess what, then I can make the earth explode by wig-
gling my ears, and we laughed like crazy, even more than the
joke was worth, just because we were jealous of Michelle Pfeiffer, who managed to get herself kissed by Emilio Rodriguez
before he died and we stopped laughing.

We always watched the end of that film dead seriously, we
always felt personally concerned because all three of us knew
what it meant to come from a rough neighborhood, where
after dusk people came out to deal crack even with little kids
and where it was always so hard to be a girl. And when Coralie
told us that her father had translated the lyrics to *Mr. Tam-*

bourine Man and that in fact it's about a drug addict who's looking for his dealer, we nodded our heads slowly with the same sad look on our faces, yeah girls, yeah, I tell you, there are times it just sucks. And we would shove aside the huge Diddle stuffed animals to make more room on Coralie's bed, and sniffle a little and really be affected by the issues in the film, deep down. I always cried a little more than the other two because you see, it reminded me—what did it remind you of, Alice?— the neighborhood I was from, never mind if I never actually lived there, the fact that my grandmother and my horde of aunts still did, and that there were photographs of my father outside those housing projects, so okay, maybe I *personally* didn't come from the banlieue, but that was my family background, anyway.

I knew that Aude and Coralie were always jealous of the extra tears I could squeeze out thanks to my *Algéritude*, as jealous as they were of Michelle Pfeiffer, so I never missed an opportunity to shed a few here and there, or to use new words in Arabic before I condescended to pass them on, as if I hadn't just heard Mommydaddy use them the night before. And the next day you felt ashamed when you saw yourself writing two or three new words phonetically when no one, not a soul, would be prepared to say there's any point to this phonetic Arabic, but your girlfriends went ahead and wrote it down, and diligently too, because you were the one with the last name that gave you every right, that allowed all of you to start shouting yoohooyoohoo when the handsome rap singer called out, Are there any Africans here tonight?

Coralie, Aude, and I were inseparable, except when we began to accuse each other of lying about how we spent our evenings: Emilio Ramirez wasn't looking at you, since he was looking at me, you big liar, and the same as with my sisters we always tried to come up with the most picturesque insults imaginable such as hey you did your liposuction with a vacuum cleaner or you have so many bags under your eyes that when you take your bulldog for a walk he's the one who looks great. But apart from our spats we were together for all the important things like when I got my first period, sitting there in English class and I felt there's something weird going on here, and I told Coralie who handed me a napkin and Aude lent me her jacket so I could tie it around my hips and hide any blood stains that might be showing and we left class all three of us to see if that's what it was and sure enough. And I was totally proud.

Or like the time, the most important event of all, when we were in Coralie's garage and we were trying her curling iron— Why don't you have curly hair, Alice, if you're an Arab? Coco is almost as curly as you are in fact . . . And so you answered, the reply that saved your ass a hundred times in your ardent quest for Algerization, that you were from Great Kabylia and everyone knows that Kabyles are actually Bretons from way back and so you could very easily have inherited straight hair over the centuries. And anyway your cousin was blonde, I know it's weird but hey for sure it does happen, and in the garage, while we were trying the iron, Aude pointed out that it was the first time that all three of us had a *steady* at the same time. Aude said "steady" the way they do in Normandy and for years I went on saying it and all the Parisians would laugh at me but in those days it was just a normal expression and Coralie said, yeah and I said yeah and since all three of us we were between twelve and fourteen years old there was only one way this could lead: we made a stupid pact to sleep with our steadies before the end of the month.

Without a moment's hesitation, in order to seal our pact— wasn't this the finest proof of friendship that existed?—we went straight to the pharmacy to buy a box of condoms to share. We stood by the rack and looked at all the different sorts, trying to look learned: ultra ribbed, what the fuck is ultra ribbed supposed to mean? And we ended up in a fit of giggles buying this box of twelve ultra ribbed condoms since not one of us was willing to admit that she had no clue what the texture of a condom was supposed to be. And after that, you idiot, for years you thought the word "rib" sounded obscene not only because it sounded like rub but also because of the promises contained in that first box of condoms . . .

In spite of the pact we made that day, which we referred to among ourselves as the "garage thing"—yeah, we nearly went through with the garage thing but then his parents showed up—by the end of the month neither Aude nor I had done anything, and even when something *along the lines of the garage thing* would begin to happen—between Guillaume? or was it Florian? and me—I would panic and yell, Stop, stop, and grab my T-shirt from the foot of the bed and leave the place practically at a run.

So it was only Coralie's bravery that gave us cause for celebration, since on the last day but one of the month—this was April—she called to tell us that she'd done it, she'd gone through with it. So we all met in the garage and each had a beer I'd stolen from Mommydaddy's cellar and we drank to Coralie's deflowering and screamed, *the details, we want the details,* but Coralie wasn't laughing at all. She looked deadly earnest and I could tell at that point that my *Algéritude* no longer cut the mustard compared to Coralie's sexual experience and that she would now take over as head of cultural activities for our trio. I cursed myself for having run away just a few days before that, especially when Coralie told us to give her our condoms because she, at least, would be using them. Aude opened her pencil case to hand over her condoms but I said, no, I'm nearly there, and it wouldn't be a good idea to go through with it without condoms. Aude said, Make sure you're covered, and we laughed, and Coralie said, No, I kid you not, girls, it really hurts and I can't sit down, and we laughed some more, so hard we were spitting beer out our nose, then I shouted, Hey don't waste it, shit, I had enough trouble stealing these ones, so we raised our beers again to Coralie's first time, to Coralie's first two times in fact because she did it once missionary and once on top, OMG were we impressed.

What's that supposed to mean, anyway, "French nationality, whatever it takes?"

You probably never asked Mad outright what he meant, and sometimes you think you should have. To avoid getting swallowed up by the Grand Inquisition at the speed of lightning, unprepared, fear in your guts. Because to circumvent the laws regarding marriages of convenience would require nothing short of an intensive training camp where liars and counterfeiters of your ilk would all crawl through the mud together for two weeks while subjecting yourselves to a volley of cross-examinations with instructors disguised as Brice Hortefeux and Nicolas Sarkozy[1] reading out the official texts until none of the punishments they prognosticated daunted you in the least.

But you didn't ask him.

It could be that at that point it still made you laugh because you could just imagine Mad walking around with a baguette under his arm, and he wouldn't sing *La Marseillaise* all wrong anymore, and he'd decide that the Panthéon was a really impressive building instead of trying to dream up all the anagrams you could make by changing the order of the big gilded letters, and he'd watch soccer, and list the names of all the

[1] Hortefeux was minister of Immigration, Integration and National Identity under Jacques Chirac from 2007 to 2009 and became Minister of the Interior under Nicolas Sarkozy in 2009. Sarkozy was Minister of the Interior under Chirac before becoming President of the Republic in 2007. (T.N.)

départements whenever he saw their numbers on car license plates, and he'd go down in the street to celebrate on Bastille Day, and he'd wave to all the tourists on the bateaux-mouches shouting "I love Paris," and he'd stick to using the pedestrian crossings, and he might even straighten his hair and stop wearing the sort of T-shirts that neither a parrot nor your own mother could stand they were so loud.

Much mistaken, as Sherlock Holmes would have said, who for a very long time was one of your heroes.

That afternoon, I was inaugurating the Arabesque's new apartment. She had just moved to Paris together with Jérémie, her completely awesome brother—whom I hadn't seen since the lycée but who to me still embodied the non plus ultra of *coolitude* because he went everywhere with his *board* and his eyes were the color of a swimming pool for rich people.

The odds of running into him played a major part in my decision to cut my last class and help the Arabesque with her boxes instead. But he wasn't there, so the Arabesque and I drank tea while we waited for him—or maybe the Arabesque wasn't even waiting for him and it was just me. And for hours we made up for lost time with a steady stream of guess-what, and no-way, completely oblivious of the appointment I'd scheduled with Mad. So when he came bursting into the apartment, neither the Arabesque nor I were surprised; after all, he knew us, he knew the size of the Arabesque's teapots. And the treachery of her ginormous cushions spread all over the floor and where I lay sprawled, practically asleep, when he began shouting at me about some *important thing* we had to talk about, and he was *fed up Alice with all your rotten plans*, and pointing a furious finger at the Arabesque he said, You—you ought to be ashamed for monopolizing her.

—What important thing? asked the Arabesque, who ostensibly pretended to ignore Mad's index finger. Leaving him no time to reply she said, If it's about the girl the other night, Alice and I already talked about it, and she is really really hideous.

Mad shrugged, while I choked with laughter into my cup.

It could have been a really cool moment. The Arabesque was back, our trio was reunited. Just seeing them there before me I could feel the same puns lurking on the tip of my tongue, I could tell our friendship hadn't lost a thing, neither the enthusiastic discussions we used to have, nor our extreme points of view when back then Mad used to treat us like some filthy viragos without raising an eyebrow. For the first time in a very long time the three of us were together, and for once it wasn't in someone's parents' house and there were no rules about not smoking or being home at a certain time.

But clearly Mad had failed to see the genius of the moment. I made a sorry face to the Arabesque, as I extricated myself from my cushion and started picking up all the stuff spread around me.

—Right, I'm coming, for the important thing.

Mad practically dragged me by the elbow to the door because I was still giggling with the Arabesque who was cross-ing her eyes to imitate the girl from the other night, the one we'd seen stuck to Mad's mouth when we opened the wrong door, and she wasn't fully clothed either, but we both agreed we wouldn't go into that part of the scene.

Down in the street I grumbled, things like "nasty brute" and "fuck off," but it didn't take long for my happiness to get the upper hand again—happiness at seeing the Arabesque, happy to be with Mad walking down the Rue de Belleville, which is without a doubt my favorite place in my entire Parisian realm, and I started chirping on too loudly about our threesome.

And then—

—Pretty soon there won't be any threesome.

Mad said it very curtly and really fast, looking at his shoes.

And I went, What, hey wait, why, Mad, why? And I was speech-less after that, I was so astonished by his anger, this thing in his voice cutting right through my happiness.

—Sooner or later they're going to send me back.

I shook my head. No way. And then: You think I'd let them take you? You think I'd be ready to lose you now that I've just got the Arabesque back and we can finally be all three together again?

Mad didn't answer. I patted him on the shoulder a few times and said, We've always managed to get back together, right? Even when you left, we're not the sort who lose touch. I tried to laugh, too, but met only the same silence. We were almost at République by the time he finally turned around and decided to look at me.

You remember what you saw in Mad's eyes just then, your own reflection, moving, this tiny thing at the back of his pupils, and then his own terrible fear that made you want nothing so much as to hug him right there and then. Now that you know what was going through his mind, that you have heard the tide of words that was about to follow, you have concluded that his fear must have had something to do with you, that he didn't trust you enough. And that rankled.

There is a way, said Mad quickly, one way for us not to lose each other, never lose each other, so they won't send me back there, you know we can keep the story from ending, because this time if I go away we'll be like two parallel lines that never meet, but I've been thinking about all this, all night long, for a few days to be honest, if you were willing, if only you were will-ing, but it's really crazy, believe me I don't want to be rude going about this, babe, I know you have thousands of other solutions, if you take it as an insult that'll be awful but I've got this stupid hope that you might like the idea, and it might even make you laugh, you know . . .

—What, Mad?

—Alice, Alice, I never thought I might ask you this some day, and it's really weird, but I don't want to leave, I want to stay here, if they send me back this time I'll kill myself or I'll kill someone, oh shit maybe you'll think this is blackmail, I figured, I figured that if you were prepared to be a circus rider with me when we were six years old, and I hated your little ruffled skirt even though you were so proud of it, you called yourself Esmeralda, a real gypsy, so could you, I mean, can you see your way to helping me, I'm ashamed to go about it like this because maybe you'll actually like the idea, you used to dream about all those scenes in the movies—like when you cried in *Edward Scissorhands* I couldn't help but see there's a side of you that's sentimental and soft-hearted and if I went down on one knee I wouldn't even have any flowers to give you, do you remember when your father said that no one could ever separate those two, and only last year you were still crying in front of the TV when they have to part at the end, and your dad was glaring at me because I was still sleeping in your room and your mother agreed with him about the film and said no, *nothing or no one* and you said this film is sad stop laughing and when we were at the dinner table I was looking at you and we were smiling with this sort of burning pride and thinking *no way, nothing, no one* and thinking too about the joint we'd smoke at the window like we always do and your eyes just then, Alice, it was your eyes the way they were just then that made me think that you might say yes and I could finally go ahead and ask you, and then there was the time by the canal when that guy called me Bamboula and you leapt up just like that to go and push him and say, What did you say? I thought about it all night and this morning I said to myself that if the next person who came into the store was blond or brunette or fat then I'd go ahead with it, and even though he was two whole heads taller than you Alice you leapt up and I can see it now, and I just don't know how to say it, no I don't know, I've been thinking about it for two whole weeks, and then there was the day when you said *I never had a brother,* and I still don't know how, we're the best friends in the world, we've never had any problems, I mean all those kinds of problems between guys and girls we've always been above all that, *I'll be your brother* I said, when we were sharing the same comforter and our skin would touch but we never felt embarrassed or anything like that, your father didn't like me all that much when he said "those two," your eyes were glowing with pride but you were never even the least bit embarrassed, no, because we're a perfect pair and you remember when one of your ex-boyfriends said that physically it wasn't possible because if a guy and a girl share the same comforter and they're right up next to each other the guy'll get a hard on no matter what and we both gave him this scornful laugh because we both knew that he could never ever understand the kind of friendship we have, *I'll always have Mad* you said when your mother told you off for splitting up with the guy again and maybe no one can understand because there has been all the Great History of Racism—Bamboula, and a split-second later you were on your feet—and all the hours we've spent side by side, and when the plane landed this last time I swore I'd never leave again, nothing or no one Alice, you split up with that guy almost immediately afterwards because that hard-on he wanted to make part of our friendship, that was vulgar, only it's not just a separation we're talking about here you and me, it's on the level of a whole country, it's between me and France, so I won't go down on one knee, *I never had a brother* you looked so sad in your skirt and your ruffles but *I'll be your brother*, my little girl, my proud little princess, and what I'm asking you now is to give me a place to drop anchor, so I can stay with you, my sister, my country, I need you, I need your country, your French nationality, give yourself to me, give me who you are so I never have to leave again, so even if this is the weirdest thing I've ever said

to you please, please, listen to me seriously, before you burst
out laughing, think again about why I have to ask you, oh shit
I'm so scared, my little one, nothing or no one, you said *I dare
you to say that again and I'll knock your head off*, if you lash
yourself to my name, you have to press with all your weight on
me, on my name, so that I'll never go away again, I told you it's
ridiculous with his hair and his scissors at the end of his hands
but you said stop laughing, Mad, it's so sad they have to part
and *I never had a brother* so don't shout, don't call me names

I'll count to three

two

one

Alice it's just two stupid words, that's all

but please

MARRY ME.

The problem with middle school, the really big problem—obviously not the only problem because you can't forgive yourself for anything these days, your way cool look or your utter hypocrisy regarding your *Algéritude* would be enough for you to look back on middle school as a sort of hell, *in hindsight*—the problem was that you and your friends were the only ones who dreamt of being Algerian, and even though it was a small school, it was kind of tough to be the three of you against the rest of the world. Especially at the age of thirteen.

The others couldn't care less about our ethnic concerts or our love for the guys on mopeds from the urban development zone next door. The others just could not see how fucking sexy Emilio Ramirez was as he sat rocking back and forth on his chair giving his personal particulars to Michelle Pfeiffer. And for the first time I heard the word Arab mispronounced on purpose, with so much venom, as if the mispronunciation were a separate word meant to hurt. And I was the one who was targeted. I got beat up for real by three older girls who came to wait for me outside the school and they said, It's unbelievable, only—how many?—three or four fucking A-rabs in this school, and still they have to go showing their fucking A-rab faces and stirring up shit. You can bet I kept quiet, I didn't hit anyone, because I was too afraid they'd drag me along the sidewalk and hit me even harder.

Because for the time being everything was fine, for the time being I was just outside the school with the head girl making sure they were hitting me just the right amount, making sure I didn't start bleeding out of my ears, and she looked at me when the other three let go of me at last, and I had snot all over the lower half of my face from sobbing, and my cheeks were all red from their slaps and my ponytail clip was over to one side because they'd been yanking my hair all over the place, whole fistfuls of it, and that hoe of a head girl, what a hoe she was, I can still see her face, her name was Céline, that hoe stood there looking at me without a trace of compassion on her face, calm and serene, and she said, You shouldn't have provoked them, Alice, it serves you right.

When I got home I didn't say anything, at dinner I didn't say anything, I had a stomachache, they had threatened to come back the next day and the day after that and on and on, we'll be your worst nightmare, fucking A-rab, and I could have told Mommydaddy, I could have told them that they were waiting for me at the gate to the school, the female version of some Doc Martens skins, just to smash my face in, my A-rab face, and I could have told them that I was sorry I ever said *bougnoule* and ask them to take me out of that shit-faced school and away from this shit-faced racist Boonville countryside, and to speak to the principal, and tell him that I know who ratted on me to those three girls and it was actually a friend of mine, or rather a former friend, and she did it because I made fun of her in a really nasty way, I agree, but then why didn't they punish me for having humiliated her instead of punishing me because I was an A-rab, one of only three in the whole school, and because I had a map of Africa at the top of my stomach, and because I'd shown it to that girl only a week earlier and she'd shown me a heart-shaped hickey she had on her neck.

But I didn't say a thing all through dinner, I'd fixed my ponytail in the schoolbus and wiped my face, I told everyone I'd fallen down during gym and I was aching all over, I said that it was just a day like any other day. I even tried to find some mean things to say about the head girl, I made up a story about how she insulted a student but Mommydaddy didn't seem to notice. I wished I could convince them that that skank Céline—who deserved the number one word-you're-not-ever-supposed-to-say and who even deserved the all-time top five insults—that bitch, hoe, slut, motherfucker, asslicker Céline deals drugs in the schoolyard and I wished my parents would go inform the police, the FBI, and Mulder and Scully, and that the very next day they'd all show up to arrest her, that they'd shout *Nobody move* and they'd grab her and tie her up and smash her face onto the hood of their car with the flashing light and handcuff her and shove her in the car and I'd go over to the open window and look out and see her face covered in snot and blood and tears and her hair hanging all down her face and she wouldn't be able to tuck it behind her ears the way she does, one of her oh so prim little gestures, and I'd say to her in a splendid bass voice, the husky sort, Marlene Dietrich's voice: You shouldn't have provoked them, Céline, it serves you right.

Instead, I said that during study hall she had insulted a boy who was making noise and she told us porn stories instead of letting us work, yes these really disgusting stories with loads of words no parent would ever want to hear crossing their children's lips, but I stopped before I could really get going because Mommydaddy said, in a really stern voice, Alice, and then they made a face tucking in their lower lips, and I knew that my face, the one I always made when I tried to imitate people's voices and which annoyed Mommydaddy because it was an ugly face, and if I went on making it they would send me off to the speech therapist without further ado, so because of the face I made Mommydaddy didn't listen at all to what I was saying but just looked at my mouth with a worried frown, wondering if I'd ever manage to get rid of that confounded face which made me look really retarded. Mommydaddy even told me so one day, although they did apologize afterwards.

So I kept my mouth shut through the rest of dinner, I was dead annoyed, then I hurried back to my room where I could bang on the walls and talk to my posters, particularly the Spice Girls, and most particularly the black girl in the Spice Girls who wore panther boots, and I asked her if she'd been through this shit as well, if she'd had her own version of skinhead Doc Martens skanks during high school and if she got beat up so hard she bled, not a lot of course, but just enough to stain her way cool outfit.

On the poster the Spice Girl had this huge smile and she was holding her friends' shoulders and I couldn't stop wondering where Aude and Coralie had been and why they didn't come and help me, with their silver boots and star-spangled bikini tops while I, the black Spice Girl, undaunted by their chains and their motorbikes, was fighting like a fury to throw off an entire army of skinheads and at the end of the fight you stepped over your enemies' gigantic inert bodies and their big black dogs and you just stood there like that holding each other's shoulders and smiling and not giving a damn about the bloodstains because as a Spice Girl of course you had your own gigantic dry cleaner's in your English country home and then you jumped up and clapped your hands and shouted, *Girl power* and shouted, *I wanna ha, I wanna ha, I wanna really really wanna zig a zig ha.*

But that's not what happened, it didn't happen like that at all, and since you were ashamed you didn't fight back, or even try to fight them off, and you didn't hit anyone, not even once, and you ran into the bathroom and took out your nail file and filed the nails of your index fingers into a point, you filed them really really pointy and you swore that next time you would tear their eyes out, and to punish yourself for being such a coward you scratched your own arms and you scratched your legs and then you also drew a frame around your map of Africa.

Mommydaddy have always been an indissoluble entity, one head with smooth hair and the other frizzy, and they share the same jokes, the same taste in solid wood furniture, and weekends by the seaside when it's very cold out and they can walk all alone along endless beaches. You call Mommydaddy Choupi, regardless of whether you mean the smooth head or the frizzy one, and they call you Little Kitty. They do the cooking, alternating between couscous and tarte Tatin, and they drink cocktails on Friday evening to celebrate the end of the week, systematically pouring out a glass of Muscat and a rum cordial. Mommydaddy are all of a piece and they kiss in front of you no matter how much you yell with disgust.

Except the night I told them Mad and I were getting married.

I came back from Paris to tell them about my decision, and Mad suggested that maybe he should come with me to ask for my hand in a totally official way, but I reminded him that there had been a time when Mommydaddy slapped his face because he'd said "fuck" at the dinner table and that he wasn't necessarily safe from a second round.

We sat down in the living room around the traditional Friday night drinks, and I too had been entitled to a glass of Muscat over the last few years even though Mommydaddy think I drink it far too quickly. So they said, What's new? And as a rule I would reply, Oh, not much, and then we'd talk about the house by the seaside, and the cats, and say how much we missed each other and how people made fun of us because we were like the perfect family in one of those cereal ads on television. But this time, between the house and the cats, I told them that there was something new, and I'd like to talk to them about it, so Mommydaddy raised their inquisitive eyebrows, already finding this entertaining, waiting for me to announce yet again that I had met *the most gorgeous guy on earth* and then off I'd go pursuing some new dream of eternal love that would last two months.

I said: It might seem a little strange to you, but I've given it a lot of thought, and I hesitated for a long time, too, but now I'm sure, and I'm going to go through with it no matter what, even if it does mean a lot to me to have your approval and support. I, I mean we, I mean Mad and I, are going to get married.

Mommydaddy, who at this point were still an indistinguishable unit, suddenly choked on a sip of alcohol and said, I beg your pardon?

—We're getting married, Mad and me, sometime this year if we can.

—But you . . . Are you? I mean . . . are you in love?

Second difficult announcement: Absolutely not. I explained to Mommydaddy that I really wanted to help Mad and that his situation had become unbearable. I told them about the Préfecture, and the residence permits that never lasted, and the nationality. I told them that if one day Mad were to be expelled from France on a charter flight to go back to a country that meant nothing to him beyond the memory of his dead father and two years of backbreaking work, I would at least like to know I'd done everything in my power to prevent it.

I recited to them everything I'd read on the internet, how Mad would be granted a residence permit unrelated to work which meant they couldn't deport him as long as he had a French spouse living in France, and how he'd be entitled to apply for French nationality, not right away of course but after four years, but since his first application had never gotten any-where maybe this would increase his chances.

And at that point Mommydaddy exploded, split in two right before my eyes, on the one hand Daddy screaming, You are out of your mind, young woman, and on the other, Mommy just sitting there silent.

Daddy, who yet again was wearing brown shoes with navy blue trousers, since he's color-blind, was shaking his head furi-ously and asking if you had really thought it through, because not only was the whole scheme completely illegal but also you would have to stay married for four years to someone you weren't in love with, and what would you do if you met another guy who wanted to hook up with you, huh, would you say sorry I'm not free because I'm committed to this completely stupid, forbidden relationship, with an expiry date four years from now?

I answered that of course I'd thought about it, what did he think I was, an idiot? But that I'd concluded I'd never be attracted to someone who didn't understand the situation in the first place, and besides, marriage wasn't really my thing, and anyway Mommydaddy themselves weren't even married, Daddy ought to understand, he was the one who brought you up with that hunger for freedom and scorn for matrimonial convention, right? So it wasn't as if Mad were occupying some-one else's place.

As for the illegality of the procedure, that was completely relative. The more I thought about it, the more I was con-vinced that this marriage—to someone I loved and respected, and with whom I'd spent nearly my entire life, was probably no more fraudulent and ill-advised than a marriage between a couple taking the plunge after they've known each other only a few weeks, and who would get divorced almost immediately afterwards.

So Daddy said, This has to be the most insane cockeyed scheme you have ever come up with.

I had figured that telling them wouldn't go all that smoothly, but when I saw Daddy's categorical look I felt like I was in some remake of *Guess Who's Coming to Dinner* in the scene where Sidney Poitier realizes his future mother-in-law is about to faint because she's discovered he's black and, classy as can be, he says, You ought to sit down before you fall down. And I was hurt to see how completely foreign my point of view was to Daddy.

I told him I was disappointed and that I had thought he would show more support for my gesture, and I told him that after the antiracist upbringing he'd given me and all his grand principles of solidarity I'd hoped he'd understand or at least encourage me and then I made the mistake of saying, Particularly coming from you, Papa.

—What do you mean particularly coming from me? Tell me, Alice, you mean because I'm an Arab? And so what? Are we supposed to all stick together because we're foreigners who've come to France, yeah sure, so we can share all our memories of racial harassment? You know what? I should go down in the street and find everyone else and tell them I have three daughters who are of a marriageable age and they're French through and through and what are you waiting for, why don't you marry them and get yourselves out of your unbearable situation? Step right this way, my doors are open, make yourself at home, any bed you like! Is that what you want, Alice? We could start a union of Blacks and Arabs who are prepared to do anything to get naturalized, and then why don't we start shoplifting too while we're at it, to punish the French for sticking us in ghettoes, that would be perfectly normal, no?

—I didn't say that! Stop treating me like an imbecile!

—Because you're behaving like an imbecile! I can't believe it, with all those years of studying behind you, that you don't have a little more common sense! You want to know what I think, Alice? First of all, I was born French, contrary to what you might have liked to think, or wished, ever since you went through that stupid identity crisis of yours. I don't know anything about Mad's problems, and I don't understand them: there's nothing about me in particular that makes me better equipped to understand that sort of problem than your mother or anyone else for that matter, so don't go labeling me with some "particularly coming from you" tag. All that I can see is that you want to do something that is illegal, that you're throwing away every chance we've ever given you to have a normal life—no, better than that, a successful life. Why can't you just make the most of what you've been given instead of wanting to go looking for trouble?

—Because I don't want a normal life!

Daddy was on his feet now, getting madder and madder, and he said that sure, I didn't want a normal life because I didn't know how much it cost them to give me that life, I just took it for granted, no sweat, no effort involved, and that it was boring. But I had no idea how hard he had struggled so that his daughters could lead that normal life, how much they had hesitated when it came time to choose our names, wondering whether an Arabic name would be a handicap, and how they had to push me in my studies so I'd be the best, so I'd have every option open to me, the same ones offered to the pure French, more options than most of them would ever have, and how overjoyed they were every time one of us was successful—when Dad read my name in the paper or on the list on the double glass door of the École Normale Supérieure,[1] but they'd been afraid, too, whenever you tried something new, and Dad would get up in the middle of the night to make sure the school really did accept stu-

---

[1] One of the most prestigious schools of higher education in France, equivalent to Harvard or MIT, preparing graduates primarily but not exclusively for service in government and science. (T.N.)

dents with foreign names and he'd go feverishly through the
list of admissions on the internet and calculate percentages,
and how he'd been afraid that the police might give me a hard
time because of my family name, and how happy he was to be
able to believe that none of us had never been judged by our
looks, and how they'd saved to be able to pay for me to live in
Paris and have an apartment and all the things he'd never had
precisely because he knew that being poor was probably more
discriminatory a factor than being an Arab so he did everything, absolutely everything, so that this normal life would
unfold effortlessly before the eyes of his three daughters. And
now I, Alice, I was sweeping it all aside, taking it for granted
as if it had been there for generations, as if I were some *grande
bourgeoise* toff who, in the end, would rather slum it, but
don't you see, don't you get it Alice, you belong to the first
generation to have a normal life, and it was your Dad's generation who had to fight for it?

You knew he was right, you knew the effort it had cost your
Dad, you didn't want to deny that. You had seen how happy
he'd been, and heard him shout for joy when you passed all
your admissions tests. You knew that Dad was never happier
than when he realized his daughters were no longer faced with
linguistic, cultural, or economic barriers, that they were free
to be upwardly mobile in this country however they saw fit,
and the higher they went, the prouder Dad would be, and
proud of himself, too, for this was his just reward. You always
thought that becoming President of the Republic would be
the most beautiful thing you could give Dad in exchange for
everything he'd done for you. Dad chose to make you a
Frenchwoman so that you would feel at ease in the country
where you were born and even though, true enough, during
your quest for *Algerization* you may have cursed him for that,
you had to admit that he had made life easy for you, you didn't
get beat up, or spat at, or turned away, and your life didn't look

at the color of your skin either, you led the life of a little white princess.

So I tried to explain to him that it wasn't that I was rejecting everything he had given me, not at all, on the contrary, I wanted to be able to do the same thing for Mad, to unroll the same red carpet, reach out with the same welcoming arms, and support him and encourage him and be a crutch for him and help him to be upwardly mobile. I said to Dad, You know there's nothing in Mali for Mad, you've seen him here with me so many times, his life is here.

And finally Mom emerged from her silence to tell me to do what I wanted to do. Dad froze, and asked her what the hell she was talking about.

Mom said she wasn't about to let some Nazi laws deprive her daughter of her best friend, and I was right to fight so that he could stay with me. She said I too had the right to belong to a generation that fought for its beliefs because, contrary to what he might think, the fight did not end with Dad. So much the better if he'd been able to obtain his own personal victory over society, but his daughters couldn't spend their entire lives carrying the banner that was proof he had won. I had to decide all on my own whether to rest on the laurels that Dad had won for me without my even noticing, or whether I should take up my own fight. Because the struggle was not over, far from it, the struggle would only be over when everyone who wanted their place here had found it, and Mom said, It's in the Declaration of the Rights of Man, no one has the right to deprive someone of his nationality or the right to change his nationality. Dad muttered, What is going on here? Is this still fucking 1968? And Mom said, No, it's fucking 1940! There is all this bullshit going on out there, and no one is lifting a finger? Genetic testing? A "detail of History?" "Selective immigration" on the basis of the candidate's IQ?

At this point in the conversation I felt I could no longer

speak because from then on it was just between the two of them. When I went up to bed three hours later I could still hear Mom shouting, But that kid is French and you know it as well as I do. And while I was trying to fall asleep not too successfully I could hear Dad's voice coming through the floorboards and he was asking her to stop making him feel guilty and hell no it had nothing to do with protecting the Jews during the Second World War and of course he would hide Mad if it came to that, even if it was against the law, and if Mom had been a little more militant in networks outside the house she wouldn't be bringing her activism into the living room and encouraging her daughter to get herself involved in an illegal, clandestine resistance movement.

You didn't know exactly what they had said to each other, although you supposed they must have stayed up very late that night. But you knew when you went down to have your breakfast in the morning, in your Dalmatian pajamas that were too small, Mommydaddy was once again a two-headed entity sitting over a double mug of coffee without milk or sugar. Mommydaddy watched you coming and they grumbled a bit and then they smiled and, biting into their bread and butter, they said, Little Kitty, it may not be the smartest thing you've ever come up with, but if you feel you have to do it, then go ahead.

You poured yourself a big bowl of cereal with only a tiny pool of milk so the flakes wouldn't go soggy too quickly, and you were utterly radiant, as if your smile had hooked itself onto your cheekbones and didn't want to let go. You felt as if your chest were being filled with enormous inhalations of love, almost unbearable in this half-asleep state you were in, because Mommydaddy was still the hero you had always imagined, the legendary warrior against racism, the valiant defender of freedom, and with them by your side you would be able to make mincemeat of the legions Brice Hortefeux would surely send out against Mad and you. Oh yes, Mommydaddy was the white knight of white marriages. And you were their Little Kitty.

—But tell that idiot not to show his face around here too soon or he'll get another slap.

As always, they were just the way you had hoped they would be.

In keeping with a family tradition that they repeated for all three daughters, Mommydaddy took me to Paris for an entire weekend, at some point during the despised era of secondary school. I was allowed to choose the places I wanted to visit, and I was given almost unlimited credit for ice cream.

I'd been looking forward to those two days for weeks, asking all my friends what they would want to see if they were in my place; that way I was sure they'd be totally jealous when I got back.

We got there on the Friday evening and I was so happy to have Mommydaddy all to myself, and to be able to choose the restaurant, and to order *two* desserts and no starter because for once we could forget about the dietary requirement of *cooked and uncooked* as Mommydaddy called it. We went to see the natural history museum, and saw the stegosaurus that stands watch over the entrance hall, and I said he looked really mean with his plates on his back but Mommydaddy reminded me that they didn't serve much purpose other than to intimidate the Sharptooths so they wouldn't attack him. Little Kitty, the stegosaurus had to look mean if he didn't want to get devoured, because other than his plates he didn't have any claws or teeth, and no legs he could run away on. And you remembered the lesson that well that ten years later, whenever you felt afraid when you were walking home at night, you would pretend to drool, and roll your eyes, and look like a terrible psychopath so you'd dissuade any passers-by from coming up to you.

We walked up the Rue Buffon singing Gypsy the Spider and I squeezed Mommydaddy's hands very tight.

We set off in the direction of the Trocadéro—certainly not to see the Eiffel Tower, which I pretended to despise in hopes of seeming more like a real Parisian—but because I wanted to go to the Musée de l'Homme. I loved models with costumes from different countries and the life-size scenes from everyday life where you could see them cooking and weaving and tanning. I commented on each of the scenes in a very loud voice because I wanted the other visitors to notice me and find me exceedingly smart, so Mommydaddy would be proud of me. I made up names for the food they were preparing and said, Oh, yes, of course it was made from corn, I read it in my book about Indians, and they could shape it like a . . . like a star, that's what it said. And it worked: a man said to Mommydaddy, What an adorable little girl, and his wife added, And she's so smart, while I puffed myself up, not trying at all to be discreet.

When you think back, it's terrible to discover that your problems with megalomania had already started back when you were only ten years old.

It was a perfect day, with a chocolate-blackcurrant ice cream to round it off, like on any other perfect day. I don't recall exactly how we got there, completely by chance, a round piazza with a golden statue in the middle surrounded by sprays of flowers, and all around the statue and the flowers there was a crowd that seemed to be mostly men. I remember noticing immediately that they were all bald and I wanted to ask Mommydaddy why, when suddenly I could tell they had gone rigid. I looked up at them and saw panic in their eyes, and they were squeezing my hands so hard it hurt.

One of the bald men saw us and a gleam of astonishment came into his eyes, you could see it perfectly even from where we stood back on the sidewalk, and then there was something else, not astonishment at all anymore, something like a grimace or a smile, something you still remember because it was the most satanic expression you had ever seen, but you didn't have enough time to really study it because suddenly Mommydaddy said RUN and they were tugging you along behind them, then they practically threw you on their back because you weren't running fast enough and for ten minutes they ran, carrying you, without stopping, without listening to you, and you were shouting and weeping and saying you wanted to get down but behind you, and this you remember so clearly, you could hear those bald men shouting and it terrified you even more than Mommydaddy's inexplicable rushing away like that, these voices shouting *Kill them* and *Death to the bougnoules.*

But Mommydaddy ran so fast that no one could keep up and after a while their feet weren't even touching the ground and we practically took off vertically and I lifted my fists in the air and I could feel the wind blowing hard through my hair, and I was shouting like the boy in *The Neverending Story* when he flies away on his beautiful white dragon with ruby eyes. We flew over the Eiffel Tower and the Obélisque on the Place de la Concorde, we frightened the pigeons, and we came back down again sort of hedgehopping just long enough to clap hands with all the people who were applauding and then Mommydaddy said, Hey, wouldn't it be a good joke now to go back and see those skinheads and give them a lesson, what do you say?

We flew so fast toward the statue of Joan of Arc that all I could hear was a high-pitched whistling sound and on our way we grabbed at all the flowers and bouquets and then as we flew ever higher we bombarded the crowd with them. Even though we were so high up I could see that the skinheads were crying and falling to their knees and probably asking for forgiveness but I couldn't hear them because we were very far away and going very very fast. Hardly a second after we'd finished our weightless window shopping along the Champs-Elysées we found ourselves in Belleville and we glided through the window of the apartment that some friends had lent us for the weekend.

It was that night, after the triumph on the Place Jeanne-d'Arc, that Mommydaddy told me about the extreme far right, and the OAS, and skinheads, and the tragedy at the Charonne métro station, and France for the French, and the Arabs they threw into the Seine, and I didn't understand, and I didn't want to understand. I wanted to go on believing in flying dragons, and in the lesson we'd given all those nasty bald men, and in the boundless love that all mankind felt for us because I was such an adorable little girl and so smart so I said, But why are you telling me all this, Papa, why, didn't you see how afraid of us they were after all? We really scared them you and me, didn't we?

But Mommydaddy just shook their heads until I stopped talking about our victory and pretending to laugh, and when I fell silent altogether he very calmly picked up where he'd left off and gave me in full his own Great History of Racism.

How he was arrested ten times "by mistake."

How they wouldn't let him into nightclubs.

How people were surprised whenever he'd start talking about a book he'd read.

And how many times did people start up a conversation with him to talk about couscous or their vacation in Tunis. One time they asked him if he had a harem. Another time during lunch break at a seminar a colleague handed him a sandwich with a laugh and it was filled with ham.

How often he had to fight.

The time his barber asked him if he would like "something a bit more European."

And one day, you remember this vaguely, someone smashed the windshield and wrote *A-rab go home* on the fender of the car.

How many people said to him, "You're not like that, but

otherwise Arabs in general, good luck trying to get them to do any work."

And I got more and more red in the face with the kind of terrible rage I used to go into when I was little and that really burned my skin and eyes and above all my ears, and I said, They all deserve a beating. But instead of agreeing with me, Mommydaddy shook their heads again, and waited for me to calm down, and then they explained that violence has never resolved anything—unless someone is picking a quarrel with you and there at least you have the right to defend yourself, you see, Little Kitty, don't let them walk all over you, either— and if you smash their face in, people like that—and most of the time they deserve it, I'll warrant you that—it will only rein- force their belief that Arabs are antisocial and criminal and dangerous.

In reality, all those people who were threatening us and shouting at us to go home were simply frightened because they didn't know us and they were afraid of us, it was as simple as that, but over time they would learn to get to know us and they would understand that we can all live together and work together and marry each other, and that there is no gap between nations. Then Mommydaddy, as was often the case, got a little bit carried away and started quoting Shakespeare by heart and saying, *If you prick us, do we not bleed?* But you weren't really listening anymore when they started getting muddled in their tirade because there was something else you'd been thinking about for a few minutes and you finally got up the nerve to ask, But why are they afraid of us?

And Mommydaddy, who at last after all the turbulent events of the day were beginning to calm down and relax, and even smile, simply replied, "Because we are so much more beautiful than they are."

Henceforth, before celebrating the marriage, the registrar of vital statistics must interview the future spouses in order to detect any potential signs of a marriage of convenience, unless he or she has absolutely no reason to doubt that the interested parties are truly consenting. In principle, both parties shall be heard together. However, should the need arise, the registrar may reserve the right to interview each party separately. If any 'serious signs' suggest an absence of consent, the registrar may refuse to celebrate the marriage and inform the public state prosecutor thereof, who is entitled to authorize the marriage, or oppose it, or decide that the ceremony shall be deferred pending the results of the ensuing investigation. Any reprieve granted by the public state prosecutor shall be no longer than one month, renewable one time only."

That is what we read on my computer screen after a first search, and Mad asked, What do you suppose the signs of a marriage of convenience might be? And I said, If you point a shotgun at me when I walk into the *mairie*, I suppose. He laughed.

We took a good look at each other. Mad said, Frankly, girl, how can it fail, we're on the same level, we're the same age, we have the same rank. I said, What rank? He answered with a sigh, You know, the rank you give people on their looks . . .

—I have never ranked someone on their looks, you toad, it's against the theory of persons.

—Well okay, but believe me when I say we must be about in the same range.

—Which is?

—I don't know, seven, or maybe eight . . . out of ten that is, not twenty.

—I would have said less.

There was a moment of silence and we went on scrutinizing each other, making appreciative faces and nodding our heads.

I could just see the *registrar of vital statistics* ranking Mad and me to ascertain "the validity of the union" and I wondered what criteria he would use, or what Mad used for that matter.

I could picture an office in the *mairie* with a scale, a tape measure, a height gauge, a magnifying mirror, a stylist, and then the entire jury of that fucking stupid program on the M6 channel where they go looking for new supermodels. I can just see Mad and me taking turns walking in front of those people, giving them our measurements and our record times at sex, and making a few jokes, and answering a volley of questions aimed at determining our charm level—sort of like one of those tests in women's magazines where you have to circle a triangle, a square, or a star: "A man walks up to the bar and asks whether you live with your parents. You think this is 1) old-fashioned 2) cute as can be 3) you kiss him without giving him the time to finish"—or what our strong and weak points are when it comes to flirting . . .

How could anyone possibly claim they can tell whether a relationship is based on love or not? Mad's physical compatibility ranking system might point to the probability of such a relationship existing, but in no way was it any sort of reliable proof. You don't always fall in love with someone who's in your league, on your level, because that in turn is determined by constantly varying points of reference. Isn't that the very thing all those Walt Disney fairy tales lulled your childhood with—Beauty who is gorgeous and falls head over heels in love with that hairy horror Beast, or the chandelier that goes off with the feather duster, or the silent Little Mermaid, wrapped up in a ship's sail, who finds her Prince. But maybe the Beast seduced the Beauty with his money? Money can really skew something like Mad's system.

But you thought you were right, all the same: there were loads of other examples, obviously, of frogs covered with pustules, and girls disguised as boys, and old women carrying heavy burdens of wood, and Harold and Maude, and then Woody Allen kissing Charlize Theron, Julia Roberts and a whole load of actresses who were all leg and mouth and diamonds. So Mad had to be mistaken.

But he also had some examples that supported his theory, like all those teen movies that make clear to the viewer that head cheerleaders can only go out with football champions, and funny black guys with black girls who wear a pink bustier, and marginal kids who want to go to art school with the members of avant-garde rock bands. Then you have the incredible modern romance about the offspring of enemy families who fall madly in love and get married with their pictures splashed all over the cover of *Hello!* magazine. Like the Bouygues-Bolloré wedding, you remember it very clearly, how it got a full spread, with statistics about this and that everywhere, and the names of all the slebs attending, and all the articles say how *young, rich and good-looking* they were, and the papers seemed to imply that these were three infallible signs that they were made for each other. But the corollary to such assertions is that old, penniless and ugly people also flock together, as do misshapen one-eyed runts, as if it were perfectly normal that Quasimodo didn't stand a chance because according to Mad's physical compatibility ranking obviously he wasn't in the same league as Esmeralda. Your grandmother even told you that Vincent Bolloré made all his guests laugh by announcing that *this could not possibly be an arranged marriage*, for one thing because the two families hated each other, but now you see that their union was inevitable because of the three points they had in common, which meant their love was absolutely irrefutable and what started out as a potential tragedy ended up with sugared almond party favors and *yes I dos*, of course you remember it, and my grandma readjusting her glasses to take a better look at the front cover of her magazine and practically blushing with happiness for their sake. Shit, Mad knew what he was talking about after all.

But even if I were to concede that his class theory in affairs of love was true, it still wouldn't be enough to prove the existence of love itself. So what would? Underwear tangled together in a shared drawer, vacation pictures where both partners look happy, the acrid smell of sex floating in the room so they'd have to tell their house guest, No, don't go in there, for fear a condom wrapper might still be littering the floor, or when you miss each other so bad you could die and your phone bills go through the roof, and you say "we" all the time, and there are those who have no shame in calling each other my love in public and who kiss in the métro and off the métro and whenever they are waiting in line and outside the door to my building, and the ones who can't even let go of each other's hand without feeling it is like some gaping wound in their shared flesh, then there are the ones I hate, with one hand in the back pocket of their partner's trousers, sometimes even in their belt, and is a double bed really necessary because maybe couples who are madly in love have had separate rooms all their lives? Or is it that my mother would have to know him and adore having tea with him and telling all her co-workers, My son-in-law is *very* interested in quantum physics? Is it something to do with the inviolable mystery of seduction, or on the contrary merely the offhand behavior of people who've been living together for way too long? What about that scene in *Eyes Wide Shut* where Nicole Kidman is sitting on the toilet and Tom

Cruise is knotting his tie and while she's pissing he talks about their evening: everyone absolutely *loves* that scene. But when you think about it, a registrar at city hall might not really be convinced if you tell him you go to the toilet without closing the door, and maybe in his opinion the only true sign of love would be if Mad could never imagine you ever feeling that kind of urge, the only true sign would be if you were blonde with wavy hair and your mouth painted bright red, on your way to pick Mad up, wearing a raincoat and fishnet stockings and sitting at the wheel of a beige SUV.

After we'd talked for an hour Mad and I still weren't sure we'd managed to pinpoint the signs of a marriage of convenience or the criteria of love. The time we spent surfing on the web didn't yield any additional information, and Mad told me that what worried him was that they might question each of us separately. We couldn't help thinking about those windowless cells with a chair in the middle and a voice coming through a crackling loudspeaker.

So I said, I don't see what they could ask us that we wouldn't know about each other, after nearly twenty years we've been together all the time. But just as I said that, I realized that I didn't have a clue what Mad ate for breakfast because we always woke up at around noon and we got going with whatever was at hand, snacking on soup, aspirin, or tea, none of your croissants and orange juice or toast and Earl Grey routine, and at that very same instant Mad asked me what my favorite color was.

I looked at my feet and finally confessed that maybe we'd need a little bit of training but shit none of my friends or family members knew my favorite color either because I wasn't really even sure I had one and anyway you could live without cornflakes.

But you have to admit you were shit-scared all the same, because of the five years of prison and the fine of 15,000 euros that you were risking, that's what you read on the websites between the brightly colored pop-ups on either side with ads for Meetic where Ingrid who was 33 and loved swimming was looking for a man between 27 and 40 with whom she could share her interests. And you thought that maybe it would be a good idea to start taking notes, learning each other's dates, and going to Ikea together to check out your household furnishing compatibility, and when you shared your thoughts with Mad he said, Yeah, and above all we'll have to come up with how many times a week we fuck.

—You think their interrogation could get as detailed as that?

—I have no idea, Alice.

—I mean, otherwise, we just say . . . five, and that should do it, no?

But if ever they did get more detailed, if ever the Grand Inquisition of Love felt the need to establish an inventory of sexual positions, if ever they verified the authenticity of a union on the basis of a shared predilection for certain practices like bondage for example, or suppose the fact we both replied "five" automatically might signal a prior agreement on the number and not an authentic passion at all—because "when you love you don't keep count"—and suppose they asked us for the names of our future children, or whether I preferred briefs or boxers, or whether Mad liked lace—I mean, who decided what constituted clues to a marriage of convenience?

Mad shared my concern and told me that maybe this marriage wasn't such a good idea after all and I saw him glancing again out of the corner of his eye at the line that was threatening me with the 15,000 euros and five years in prison and only one week prior to that we had seen a documentary on television about this prison for women where the inmates disfigured the newcomers using the sugar lumps they kept in their pockets after meals.

But Mad had always been there, remember, Mad told S. that he'd make him *eat the sidewalk* the next time he st-st-started messing around with me, and Mad drove me to the seaside in his parents' car one night when I was depressed, and Mad was fed up with his temporary residence permits and all the hassle with his papers, and Mad didn't want to go back to Mali where his father had died, and Mad was entitled to whatever I could give him so I said, No, we can't just give up.

I told him that it was just too early to talk about sex, we still had our coffee cups in our hands, and the night before, Jérémie had given a concert, and anyway watch out, I said, you're splashing coffee onto the computer keyboard, you're going to ruin it, let's just plan a few meetings where we can talk about all this, lace and babies and erogenous zones, what about tomorrow evening? And Mad replied, what about every Thursday evening for a while, just whatever it takes. I held out my fist, we made a deal, and from then on one evening a week I went to Mad's place with a bottle of Muscat, or Mad came here with some wine and we went through every detail one after the other, everything we could possibly imagine that might cross the mind of a particularly nitpicky, or obsessed, *registrar of vital statistics.*

He came back from Mali just at the beginning of the lycée. At the end of the month of August, when I'd already bought all my school notebooks and a diary with a way cool message to let the world know I was way cool, there was Amadou outside my door in a huge green T-shirt that said *Los Angeles City of Angel* with a dead obvious absence of the "s" at the end of the word.

He'd grown, it was incredible how much he'd grown, and so had I. But I had also developed, horizontally so to speak, and this meant that the first time we saw each other again we might feel really awkward and not recognize the little kid we used to play with anymore, because it was incredible how many inches puberty had added to my chest and hip measurements and to Amadou's shoulders, but as soon as he came over to me and tapped me on the shoulder he said, Hey, Snow White, you look almost like a girl now, too bad it's all fat, and I answered something like, You can talk when you've managed to get a suntan on the palm of your hands, loser, because I am, by far, dude, by far *your finest girlfriend, even finer than the finest of all your girlfriends,* and Amadou went, Wow, what a reference, and we entwined our fingers in this complicated way we would work on all through the lycée until we finally got it down just like in that fucking "Good Morning Vietnam" and it became our morning ritual but now I've forgotten it.

Instantaneously my best friend ever was once again my best friend ever, which was perfect timing, because I wasn't talking to Coralie or Aude anymore. Coralie went out with Emilio Ramirez behind our back at the end of the tenth grade, and after a decisive shouting match Aude and I tried to go on just the two of us but it just didn't work out she was such a moron and she wouldn't lend me any of her clothes. So even though Amadou didn't bring me back a drum—and on top of it he said, But Alice, that is such a racist vision of Africa, maybe you thought I'd bring you some pictures of me and my family outside our hut too? Which proved not that I was a racist but that he had sort of forgotten about me during those four years because he'd also forgotten that I wanted some giant drums for the band I was going to be in; but in spite of the slight, hurtful distance that had come between us, Amadou and I started hanging out together again. We were together in class and between class, and then every Friday and Saturday evening. Since we didn't live on the same side of town, we were forever riding our bikes to get to each other's houses and I hated that bike ride because on the bypass there was a steep bridge where I always had to get off and push.

In the beginning, of course, Mommydaddy were worried about my relationship with Amadou because we often slept together in the same bed when we got home from parties and no way were Mommydaddy going to tolerate my initiation into sexual life under their roof. Amadou thought this was hilarious and when he came to my house he always deliberately left disturbing clues for my parents, like going into my underwear drawer and scattering panties all around the bed, or writing "condoms" on the shopping list posted on the kitchen wall.

In fact both of you thought that as far as accusations went it was practically incestuous and never ever would you have thought there was anything ambiguous between the two of you, even when you shared the same bed, or he came into the bathroom while you were having your shower to shout, Move it, woman, we're late.

We spent our evenings talking about Boris Vian and legalizing marijuana, and we watched *The Wall* at least a hundred and fifty times, and we wrote screenplays for short films about zombies, and a really rabid critique of consumer society, and we would play at turning off the volume on the TV so we could rewrite the dialogue, while we were sneaking drinks from the bottles at the back of the liquor cabinet, and of course we could not fail to see ourselves as the center of the universe and THE cultural reference.

The first year of lycée Amadou changed his name to Mad Dog for no other reason than that it sounded classy, and since I'd never managed to come up with any sort of decent nickname I was jealous. Not one of the nicknames I'd tried had ever stuck, I mean at least the ones I liked and was proud of and that sounded so much more modern than Alice, like "Z" which went on to become your tag and got grafittied on the walls with a Posca pen and onto the tables with the point of a pair of dividers, Z stands for Zeniter, ta-dum . . . At the end of the day the only names that stuck were those little family endearments like Kitty, Oudelali, or even the way my big sister called me Uncle Al because of some obscure childhood game where she was the rich cotton planter and I was her black servant, and naturally what the game consisted of was me washing tidying serving brushing scratching braiding entertaining all to a soliloquy about my condition as a slave while I was supposed to dream up all these plots to overthrow my sister, which always failed. So I never got to be the rich cotton planter. And when you have to explain to people why your sister still calls you Uncle Al and where it came from, you can tell they think your game is unbelievably warped and you cannot fathom how or why you made up this game instead of going on calmly playing Fantômette the masked superheroine with the pomponed black satin bonnet that Mommydaddy went to so much trouble to make for you.

So all those years at the lycée there was Mad Dog, there was me with no nickname, and there was the Arabesque.

She joined our very elitist circle after a history class at the beginning of our penultimate year. We were learning all sorts of bull about the origin of religions and, apart from the lesson on Islam where you raised your hand to recite the five pillars, dead proud of your big mouth, Mad and you weren't really paying much attention and you sat there drawing crucifixions as seen from above because it was something Dalí had done and you were really into Dalí in those days, more than any other painter, even more than Gauguin who you'd loved for years because he painted women who looked like you—except for the breasts, said Mad to piss you off, and you said, Hang up, dude, you've got no dial tone.

So the girl sitting in front of us turned around and she had big blue eyes that normally would be cause for discrimination on our part, but her hair was all over the place and she was wearing baggy trousers, so we hesitated on how to classify her. And she said, Honestly, I'm fed up with all this bull about Jesus. And we went, yeeeaah, a little wary all the same. You want to hear something about Jesus, she asked. Yeeeaah. So she began telling us this joke I'd already heard, because Mommy-daddy had told it to me maybe two hundred and fifty times over, about how Christ and Mary Magdalene met. Except that when Jesus said, He that is without sin among you, let him first cast a stone, a huge boulder came down and crushed Mary Magdalene, and Jesus turned around and said, Hey, Ma, don't you think you're exaggerating a little? Mad looked at me before laughing at the end of the punch line—because you really did everything together, even to the point of deciding what was supposed to be funny—and with a big smile I said, My father loves that joke. The Arabesque said, Mine too, and after that day she began to hang out with us.

Since that joke had been our first common ground, we used

to go around saying, "He that is without sin." We took it to extremes, such as, "Oh, it's yummy, he that has never spilled spaghetti Bolognese on his neighbor, let him complain about the state of his T-shirt," or "He that is without the sin of self-ishness, let him pass the joint before I ask for it, that'd be cool," and we repeated it so often that in the end it we just said, "lethim" in one word when we meant to say we didn't give a shit about something.

The Arabesque, contrary to what her nickname might suggest, isn't an Arab at all—since I'm the Arab in the group and Mad and I had already shared out the task of representing Africa above and below the Sahara. Her Mommydaddy was one hundred percent white bread, pure local produce, even though she liked to claim she couldn't be a hundred percent sure about her origins since her mother had an affair with a Moroccan engineer just after she left school so maybe he was her real father. The first time she told us that, Mad and I didn't say anything. The second time, I raised an eyebrow full of doubt, and the third time, Mad said, And guess what, my Ma is Rosa Parks, so stop bullshitting. You're white bread, okay? Lethim.

But the Arabesque wasn't happy with that because deep down she wanted to be a *bougnoule*, and she spent her time reading Khalil Gibran, Amin Maalouf, and Mahmoud Darwish. And it was because of the stuff she read that Mad started calling her the Arabesque. I wanted to call her Mîm like the first letter of her real name, which she had carved on her back, and even when you knew it was just a scar left over from an operation to remove a mole, you couldn't help but see it as a response to your own birthmark and the proof, contrary to anything Mommydaddy might say, that each of us bears the mark of our identity somewhere on our skin.

Mîm's problem was that very quickly, through a perfectly normal association of ideas, everyone started calling her "Marceau," which didn't bother her in the beginning because like everyone else I hung out with at the lycée she was a fan of street theater, and contact juggling, and tightrope walkers and guys who juggled bare-chested in the park, but the minute the strap of Sophie Marceau's ball gown slipped off her shoulder at the Cannes film festival and she *flashed her tits* in front of *thousands of television viewers* the Arabesque refused to go on using that nickname. We got together, the three of us, and decided she was right because no way did we want all and sundry to go around thinking we called her Marceau because of some middle-of-the-road French actress. Thing is, moaned the Arabesque, she can't even compare, it's not like she has even one ounce of Bardot's sex appeal.

Mad came right out and said that Bardot had turned into a racist old bitch but the Arabesque and I still maintained that before she became a ROB she'd had a heap of class, even if for no other reason than she'd had it off with Serge Gainsbourg who was really way fucking classy.

All through our years at the lycée he was one of our idols, even though the Arabesque said he had the kind of voice that goes around raping little girls. We liked to listen to him lying on the floor in my room with the volume full blast and with every deep breath Mad would snigger and the Arabesque and I would blush and look away quick as we could.

When Mommydaddy informed me that the Pope had outlawed *Je t'aime moi non plus*, our admiration increased a hundredfold, and as we conscientiously inhaled our joints we would try to imagine whether there could be anything classier on earth. I so wish it would happen to me, said the Arabesque and Mad asked, What do you mean? With your texts, or a song? You don't even sing. And the Arabesque said, all dreamy, No, no, I'd like to be outlawed, personally, by the Pope. And I said, But wouldn't it be even classier to *be* the Pope than to be outlawed by him?

It was really strange to discover that this boy whom, back in the lycée days I had initiated into the female body by describing totally without shame the location of the clitoris and giving him advice on how to apply his caresses in a certain strict order, was now almost as embarrassed as I was when it came to talking about our sexual lives for the Grand Inquisition on Love.

Even though we began quietly laughing about it, even though Mad said, Don't worry, no reason to get upset, I won't tell your mom and dad, a lot of the time we had to finish the bottle before we could actually start talking. In the beginning, especially, that first Thursday evening, it was dead hard to say the first words and to try and guess the first question they might ask, and Mad was constantly clearing his throat while I ran my hand through my hair. *C'mon, show them you're not afraid of turning on all the bandits.*

But not a word came out of our mouths; it was as if, for the first time, we were one of those dumbass couples who've hooked up after an evening of speed dating for no other reason than a desperate desire to meet someone, as if we were out on one of those first dates where you can't help but think, even for just a split second, that it would be so much easier if one of you could just come out and say, Fuck me, or I love you, instead of rambling on and on about the Peter Doig exhibition and that painting, you know, the one with the red canoe that seems to be melting into the river, that long flowing streak of paint . . .

We thought about the registrar of vital statistics, and talked about him, and gradually we began to actually see him, give him a personality, this mysterious, worrying entity; we gave a name, virtually a face, to our Grand Inquisitor. We decided to call him—her—Edvige, in honor of the software that everyone was talking about in those days and which was supposed to be a way of putting all minor delinquents on file, along with political, syndical, and religious figures—as if, said Mad, my little brother might find himself in there stuck between Mother Teresa and Bernard Thibault the union activist. Edvige stood for *Exploitation documentaire et valorisation de l'information générale,*[1] and Edvige the Inquisitor remained a man, despite his feminine-sounding name, and he lived in a room with walls covered with books and files, and stretched between the walls were clotheslines hanging with the drying photographs, only just developed, of hundreds of thousands of suspects. Edvige had red eyes from all the reading he did, and callused fingers from turning pages. Edvige had a reedy, very soft voice, almost sugary, with hardly any change in tone, terrifyingly even. Edvige was as freaky as Anthony Perkins at the end of *Psycho* where there's a fly crawling along his hand and he doesn't move, just smiles and says he's a kind man and he won't hurt it.

Edvige's disquieting presence obliged us to start on our Inquisition of Love despite our reticence to bring up certain topics, and you thought that Mad must be like you, that when a phrase stuck in his throat it was because he could see Edvige curled up in one of the empty armchairs waving his long white hands very slowly with his head sunk between his shoulders as he promised you years of prison and a huge, horrific fine, so you forced yourself, yes, you plucked every single word one by one as if you were removing a fishbone from your throat with two fingers.

[1] Documentary Use and Development of General Information (T.N.)

We started by talking about how we'd name our kids, and we argued for hours because Mad said we had to use French names to show our willingness to integrate and I said fuck no, we can lie about our sexual activity, okay, that's one thing, but no way was I about to promote the policy of colorlessness which we had attacked all through our years at the lycée. If we were sufficiently open-minded to get married despite our different nationalities and skin colors, we could easily be one of those Bohemian couples that name their kids after Indian gods and goddesses or mythological figures, besides I love the names Ulysses and Ephraim, and then of course there were all those names I'd come across in books I'd read and that were really off the wall but that I really liked, such as Enjolras or Lautréamont or a few that made me die laughing, like Knut.

Mad said it was easy for me, with my catch-all first name, to think that it might be an advantage to have an eccentric sort of name, but he didn't want Edvige the Registrar to go thinking he would choose a name that would be a burden for the child. So excuse me, but with Ulysses, everyone would go and sing, "U-sissy Ulysses" and Ephraim was like effrontery, and besides our kid would be black so to give him some Scandinavian name, how off target could you get, and he went on and on and on until finally I shouted, No, excuse me, but *our* kid won't be either black or white, or any fucking thing at all, because *our* child won't exist at all, and why couldn't we just stop going on about it and getting all worked up over something hypothetical that nothing could harm, even the stupidest names like Périphérique or Boulevard-Haussmann with a hyphen in the middle?

And every time we insulted each other, every time our fear of being found out came back and painstakingly tangled our guts up in a despicable ball of yarn that not even wine could untangle, we bit our lips until they nearly bled trying not to hear Edvige's satanic laughter.

Edvige had something of Bela Lugosi about him, in his finest vampire performances, with flour for cake make-up and two triangles painted with charcoal to make his cheeks look gaunt. His weapons were not only thousands of euros and years of prison; Edvige was terrifying because he could wave before Mad's eyes the specter of detention centers and airplanes and expulsion and unspeakable living conditions and endless chainlink fences and prison visiting rooms and being escorted to the border.

Edvige was the tutelary power of the forest around the former detention camp of Sangatte, which now seemed to be plunged in almost mythological obscurity, as if it had once again become wild, unexplored terrain of the kind you first read about in Jack London, populated by ghosts and wolves, with ice cracking beneath every step you took, and those who entered that forest *would never come out again . . .*

Edvige was also the sniggering in the background that no one could hear in the evening news broadcast, but that you and Mad thought you had heard once or twice: sniggering by way of a funeral march for all those who, for lack of a homeland, committed suicide. And there were many of them. And you were keeping count.

Because you had to admit it wasn't for Mad's sake alone that you wanted to go through with it. Somewhere along the way something had shifted and you began to feel like a martyr for a greater cause, the patron saint of all the *bougnoules* and all the illegal immigrants. There was a crown of thorns growing around your head, and a halo, and maybe even nails in your hands, and you adopted a calm, suffering demeanor that turned you into a Raphaelite figure. The holy mother of all the lost souls, all the asylum seekers. You believed in it. Your Papa shouted at you every time you met. You turned your sad, dignified face to him, and he said it was enough to drive a person mad.

But how could he know. Papa never sat and watched the news with Mad. But you did. And it was getting harder and harder to finish your deluxe Quattro stagioni pizza—the one with asparagus on top—when you heard the names of John Maïna and Chulan Zhang Liu and Baba Traoré and the others: all drowned, hanged, thrown from windows, and their only land of asylum was a handful of dust to cover their bodies.

—Is that what you call the right to a homeland? asked Mad, in a rage.

And you tried to hide the little packet of spicy oil you had in your hand, because you were ashamed to be eating in front of your best friend who had lost his temper and couldn't sit still on the sofa.

One evening there was a documentary about the *harragas*.[2] I don't remember at what point Mad grabbed my hand and began squeezing my knuckles. We were watching the little television, we could see the boats pulling away, and then the wrecks that washed up out of the sea months later, and they told us how many had disappeared. The *harragas* who died with no land to call their own, out at sea, or within sight of the coast, somewhere between Italy, Spain, Morocco, France, and Melilla. And they did not know the nationality of the water that gradually entered their lungs—give or take a few feet it might have been French water, or Spanish water, and as it entered their porous skin it was the nationality they had wanted so badly, the country they had sought to reach, gently penetrating them, taking them into its embrace, drowning them. And perhaps the fish that swam toward them with their horrible hollow round mouths, with their toothless kisses, were French or Spanish, too. The *harragas* never knew, when they were sinking. And I wished I could marry all of them.

[2] North African migrants who attempt to enter European countries illegally. (T.N.)

I could not help but ask Mad, What do they think they're going to find here?

—You, said Mad, but I'll have to tell them that I got here first.

—Idiot.

Hadn't they heard, before they set off in their leaky tubs, that France didn't want them? Because it was out of the question, no way could we *make room for all the misery on the planet.* We had to leave it outside the door.

I knew why I would say *I do yes I do.* So that Edvige would never laugh at Mad, never transport him to the far side of the Mediterranean. So that Mad would never know the charter flights with their blue and white seats, and the little paper cloth for your head that they changed between each flight, whole planefuls of people being taken away by force, and maybe some ordinary passenger who would ask couldn't they give them all a shot to calm them down because she had a headache, while the policemen were clocking up their frequent flyer miles.

—Don't you think it's strange, asked Mad, that all of a sudden they're talking about all these repatriations by plane? They've been doing it for years and suddenly you find out that charter flights aren't just for going to visit Rome or Budapest for fifty euros round trip.

I looked at him and I could see from the way he held himself that he was coming up with a theory. It was like when we were ten years old and he'd play Sherlock Holmes and I'd take turns being the damsel in distress or Doctor Watson. The same frowning eyebrow, the same way of holding his head forward, the same crossed hands. Ever since we started on our Inquisition, Mad had constantly been coming up with theories. So I asked him what he had in mind.

—I think, said Mad, that this is a reaction to 9/11. Like the Arabs are paying for their sins. The airplane is the symbol. He who has killed by the plane will perish by the plane. A very biblical sort of proposition.

I laughed, then told him what I thought: Isn't your theory a little weird? And: Mind you don't go crazy with all this stuff you've got going through your head, it's getting weirder and weirder, but I'm beginning to worry about it a little, and maybe—and don't take this badly—maybe you're sick.

—I'm not sick. I'm Malian. That's a lot more harmful to your health.

During the four years we were at the lycée, Mad, the Arabesque and I carefully drew up a list of everything that was classy and everything that wasn't, of people who rocked and people who sucked. In random order, now, what was classy—and this is in no way an exhaustive list because as far as you can remember there was not one single aspect of public or private life that you did not rake over the coals— what was classy was not wearing a coat in the winter, or a belt, but a short-sleeved T-shirt over a long-sleeved T-shirt, with cords—but not that velveteen stuff, no way—and it was classy to wear moss green and brown and black and white, but no bright colors except for red, and it was classy to braid your hair pulled back tight, and to listen to Mommydaddy's records, and to organize afternoons spent painting, and to use argan oil, and to know how to spell ylang-ylang, and to take trips to Eastern Europe, and to jump up and down at concerts, and play the guitar, and learn complicated recipes by heart—but no more than that, in order to keep the feminist convictions you share with the Arabesque intact—and smoke hand-rolled cigarettes, and invent cocktails, and read Kerouac and Boris Vian, and sing out loud to yourself in the street, and show off the Africa birthmark on your belly, and to be black, and to accuse the philosophy teacher of being ethnocentric, and to walk out of his classes and shout that it was a scandal, and to use obsolete words, and to quote from Malcolm X. You had class if you used way or totally as an adverb, and if you said bro' to a girl, and you really had class if you were bisexual, by virtue of the beautiful theory that states that it's not a particular gender that you love, but a person. You had class, too, if you doubled up words, like we would do our homework *tête-à-tête*, and we liked to show off *this way and that way*, and we were always *looking for a way to find a way*, and in all things we were *ghetto-ghetto*.

You had class if you knew the names of all the heroes of decolonization. There were two reasons for this last rule: first of all it was simple because we had pictures of all those guys in our history books, and secondly because obviously too many of the privileged happy few on our list of people who rocked were white. Sartre, who turned down the Nobel Prize; the Stones; Hemingway who went off to fight in Spain, or even the Chevalier d'Éon, who was a symbol of the delicious blending of genders and whom the Arabesque adored: they were all immaculately white. It's because of the media, Mad would say, I mean you never see people of color in the media, so how do you expect Blacks and Arabs and Chinese to have any cultural impact? And the Arabesque always had to go one better by reminding us that in the collective unconscious we would never be anything more than lazy banana eaters or perfidious carpet vendors. And I said, What about the Chinese? Are they doomed to play ping-pong for the rest of their lives? And Mad spat on the floor with disgust because of the news presenters and the other French media who doomed us to ignorance.

So all three of you, with your grandiose ideas, felt obliged to combat that ignorance, or rather the culture that ignored color, the culture of colorlessness, and you read and reread the chapter in your history book, monotonously chanting the names of Lumumba and Senghor and Bouteflika, and even if he wasn't a hero of decolonization, you managed to get the two of them to venerate the great name, the thrice great name of Abd el-Kader, whom you always pictured on horseback wearing the purple burnous of the sultans, whom you imagined to typify all the heroes in your dreams, but you always went beyond what you'd read about his life, and for two or three months you lived on names out of the past, the three of you created a culture of non-carpet-vendors and non-banana-eaters and you even planned to open a branch office for non-ping-pong-players, and it was all going really well for you until suddenly the French media pulled a fast one and switched their interest to a brand new incarnation of the Arab that you had never even thought about.

On September 11 I was way too preoccupied to watch TV or listen to the radio because I was thinking about this guy that the Arabesque had introduced me to and that I really liked, and I was thinking about the way he said hello to me, and his liquid green eyes that were just slightly too far apart, and I was wondering if there would *be a way to find a way.* I was on the carpet in my room, between the little girl parrots that were still on my walls and the comforter and the coat rack that Mommy-daddy had made for me, and I was diligently writing that I thought I was in love. I dosed the hypothetical degree of the various formulas with care, because you never knew whether my sisters or a girlfriend or even The Boy himself might get their hands on this notebook someday, so I would have to be able to deny it, and I was sitting there hesitating between I think I'm falling in love and I think I'm beginning to fall in love and I think that I might actually be in love and then my big sister came home and I could hear the door slam, which made me feel sick because I didn't want her to come up while I was writing, but she didn't come up, she was shouting for me, louder and louder and when finally I came out on the mezzanine she shouted, IT'S WAR.

So I ran downstairs and turned on the TV but since all the channels were showing the same images over and over I got the impression that dozens of planes had crashed and were still crashing into towers, and I couldn't hear the commentary because I just thought it was a war on, and I was trying to find out between who and who, and it took me an hour or two to actually figure out what was going on.

The next morning was strange because that was all anyone was talking about in the yard at the lycée, but none of us had the geopolitical knowledge required, so I said, I thought it meant war, and the Arabesque said, Well, it might come to that, don't you think? And Mad said that he didn't want to talk about it all day long, I mean seriously, we're not going to go along with what the media want, that's all they're talking about right now so are we going to *let them influence us as well*?

But for sure we were influenced, a little bit anyway, and the rest of the country was no different. After September 11 it was all over, the culture of colorlessness, anyway, because there were Arabs wherever you looked on all the news channels, they showed videos where there were Arabs wearing long djellabas and turbans, and often they had machine guns, and these were the images that entered the collective unconscious and made the carpet vendors disappear. From September 11 on, those carpets hand-woven by Arabs were all suspected of hiding the secret entrance to a cave where suicide pilots were trained, where weapons of mass destruction were manufactured and where, probably, American flags were burned, and for sure sometimes they'd quote Chomsky, but that cultural reference was not enough to fill the enormous breach that had opened all along the fault lines of the Axis of Evil. The three of us had to learn to come to terms with the face of Terrorism—its long beard, its dark skin and its hate-filled cries for holy war: the face that suddenly appeared on every TV screen on earth.

It wasn't something we dealt with right away. No, initially we followed Mad's advice and stopped talking about the Twin Towers and Ian Thorpe who'd been there or who had almost been there you can't remember but it was horrible because you adored Ian Thorpe, and all those people who stayed inside right to the end and who were still hoping they'd be rescued instead of having to die after the most amazing skydive of their life, and obviously Mad and the Arabesque and you all swore that you would have jumped without a moment's hesitation, just for the thrill of the experience.

But on September 12 at noon Mad said we had to shut up about it. And the silence suited us, because in those days all we really knew about terrorism was the mythology about the Red Brigades, which kind of made us fantasize a little, and because Osama bin Laden looked handsome and we hated the American empire as a matter of principle. In those days Mad was still confused about Israel and Palestine—whose side are you on, Alice?—and the first Gulf war meant nothing to us beyond the date when the internet was invented and, as far as political involvement on the part of our avant-garde trio went, we'd gotten no further than the LAM, the Lycée Anarchist Movement, which we founded to punish the professorial and managerial milieus for the oppression to which they subjected us—they treated us far worse than that TV network director who came out and said our brains had to be made *available* so they could sell us their crap—so our activism wasn't limited just to our school but spread to our town and maybe even Basse-Normandie—but that for us was already virtually an internationalist dream.

So this LAM of ours, where we blocked the classroom doors with lockers, and stole teaspoons from the cafeteria a few at a time—fuck, we ended up with nearly a thousand—in order to demand a symbolic ransom, and liberated the stuffed animals from the science lab and decorated the hallways with toilet paper—this LAM didn't really have a platform regarding the situation in the Middle East, or large-scale terrorism, or the first invasion of the United States.

And yet it must have acted as a trigger, it was bound to act as a trigger, because a few months later, by the time the war in Iraq started, you knew the history of the Gulf War, and the Israeli-Palestinian conflict, and you knew about Afghanistan, and that there were two Bushes whom you hated no longer simply on principle but with full knowledge of the facts, and you decided that the only American president who was even remotely worth the time of day was Jimmy Carter because he had made the balance sheet of his peanut factory available to the public.

The war in Iraq managed to do what 9/11 had failed to do: wrench the three of us from the self-absorption that was our way of life and propel us into the real world. It obliged us to really read the papers, and encyclopedias, and atlases, because we had come to realize the enormity of our geopolitical ignorance. Mad would never admit it today, but for a long time he was convinced that the Middle East was somewhere between the Little East and the Great East. And I'd always thought that it was Charles de Gaulle who had decided to create the state of Israel at the end of the Second World War to make people forget about Vichy, and the Arabesque thought that Persia still existed, and the Ottoman Empire too while you're at it, in some remote part of the planet.

Because when they declared war, suddenly our paltry knowledge was no longer enough, and suddenly the idea of knowing *the* truth was no longer quite so tangible. We marched into battle for information, and to protest. Mad, the Arabesque and I were there at every demonstration, particularly as we were the ones organizing them. We handed each other floppies with the text of our fliers because Mommy-daddy's connection wasn't fast enough for us to send them to each other by email, and we'd stay up late into the night to print and cut our fliers, convinced that we were militants, resistance fighters.

We wrote: "Democracy is not required by blood," "Stupidity is a weapon of mass destruction," "I won't go to war for the sake of your SUV," "Colin Powell, you're the one cheating with the UN," and so on. In the morning we distributed our fliers outside the lycée and with the help of a megaphone that the Arabesque got from her union activist mom we called for an immediate demonstration. We went up the main street to the center of town chanting anti-Bush slogans to the theme music from *Tom Sawyer*, and even when there were only a dozen of us we felt as if we were changing the world and beating back barbarity.

It was always our same friends who came, members of Attac—there were five of them at the lycée—and some of the guys carried djembes, and there was the Arabesque's brother Jérémie and his gang of skaters, who came to demonstrate with beers in their hands and tried to hit on all the girls in the crowd.

Except you. Or not enough, you don't remember exactly, but you do remember that you had designs on all of the Arabesque's brother's friends, and on her brother too, something you never dared confess to her. You would look at them while they hung out performing tricks jumping over benches, and you'd blush whenever they looked your way, and when they really looked at you you managed to convince yourself that those looks of theirs meant something special, and when they asked you for a light you could hear indecent proposals behind their every word.

Their presence was one of the things that drove your frenzied activism and it offered a few opportunities to experiment with a new sort of existential self-interrogation: is it sexy for a girl to chant slogans? Wouldn't it be better just to write the slogan on a sign? But what if one of them wanted to take me by the hand to make a chain or something, what would I do with my sign?

You dreamt of finding the funniest, most intelligent slogan, you dreamt of bringing a halt to the war all by yourself, by coming up with *the* irrefutable argument, and with tears in his eyes Bush would beg your forgiveness, and all of the Arabesque's brother's buddies and the Arabesque's brother himself would say wow, way to go girl and they'd come to see you to tell you, Frankly Alice, you are just so, so, and I love what you're doing, I saw you right from the start, you didn't notice, it was just to distract you that I was hitting on the girl next to me because I'm really shy, but—*marry me!*

There were also two supervisors who encouraged us not to yield to pressure when the administration was telling us to get back in class, and sometimes they *ordered* us to get back in class, and one of the cooks from the lycée told us all about his youth, and of course it was the Arabesque and Mad and me who sniggered in the principal's face as we left the lycée, and we were running after people in the courtyard and asking them if they were prepared to be *accomplices* to this war and occupation, and over and over we'd say stuff like *Operation Iraqi Freedom* and *Shock and Awe* and we'd insist and say, Is that what you want, huh? And people would join us and everything was going smoothly, until the day we went to see Marie-Amélie.

We had decided that our propaganda for freedom wouldn't be a total success until we had tested it on this bitch who had stated publicly that she was right-wing. Which was the first of the six reasons why I hated Marie-Amélie:

1) She was right-wing.

2) She was so far right that her right-wing father was running for the right in the legislative elections.

3) She wore clothes that cost an arm and a leg, of the sort that made Mommydaddy shriek when you would point to them in the shop and they said, 600 francs for a pair of jeans, do you think money grows on trees, or what?

4) She was beautiful, that kind of fair-complexioned, chilly, blond beauty that I would never ever be able to dream of hav-

ing, a kind of almost regal beauty, with big blue eyes and a pure medieval forehead, and between her perfect breasts she wore a baptismal medallion with the head of the Holy Virgin who looked just like her.

5) She had this drawl when she spoke, and she paused between each word, endlessly.

We argued all the time, about everything. The most recent argument had been about abortion and of course she hadn't budged one inch from her original position, which was that abortion ought not to be allowed except in cases where the pregnancy endangered the mother's life. The Arabesque was about to kill her, or to come out and say she hoped she'd have to give birth to the child of a rapist, when the teacher came out into the hall to tell us to get back in class *right this minute* or go and explain ourselves to the principal.

Marie-Amélie was our threesome's atavistic enemy, she was our *perfidious Albion.* What we wanted wasn't even so much to win her over, because we knew she was a lost cause, but to bang her over the head with our irrefutable rhetoric and knock her out after two rounds of perfect arguments so that she would be forced to confess that she's no better than a right-wing slut. And anyway, said the Arabesque, if it weren't for her *body perfect* measurements no one would have said a word to that bitch for years, it's only because guys drool over her that she manages to have friends, and when I think that Jérémie slept with her at Antoine's party I get this pain in my butt, here.

6) She slept with Jérémie.

Mad said, No way could I sleep with some right-wing bitch, and I laughed and then I whispered, For a start you'd have to find a right-wing bitch who'd be capable of sleeping with a Black before you even ask yourself the question. The Arabesque said that was one point for me but Mad shrugged and muttered that if he wanted Marie-Amélie he would have Marie-Amélie.

So we went looking for her and found her smoking her Fine 120s outside the lycée with Eva and Caroline who I hate too because they wear boots with heels and in those days that was reason enough.

Mad said to her, Hey, aren't you going to the demonstration? Now, how come that doesn't surprise me! She went, Ha, ha, and Eva pointed her middle finger at him, looking bored. Just checking, said the Arabesque, and then she went, What? And we went, Oh, you know, just wanted to find out whether any of this bothers you, interventionism, innocent civilians who are going to suffer, lies, blood for oil, Bush, the war, famine in the world, the spread of evil, and death.

Marie-Amélie took a long draw on her cigarette and replied very slowly—I could not stand this total lack of speed that was so characteristic of her, see reason 5) above—that she wasn't at all surprised to see us show up feeling all proud of ourselves. She said, Hold it, hold it right there, if this isn't a perfect example of just how marginal you can get, you wouldn't be supporters of Saddam Hussein while you're at it, would you? No? Because if you're going to play the ethnic stupidity card . . . Saddam may be a dictator but he's an *Arab*, isn't he—normally that's enough for you. Okay, he may not be black but no one's perfect, right? You guys are pathetic. You know what, go somewhere else to abolish apartheid. You're not needed here.

Eva and Caroline sniggered. And we felt stupid because we didn't know how to answer back. Or at least not in an intelligent and politically viable way, because what we did say was Stupid bitch, and the Arabesque added, Racist skank, the day we truly do abolish psychological apartheid you'll feel like an idiot for not being a little white princess anymore. And I said, And you've got the fat thighs of a hoe in that dress.

Great.

When we left, I poked Mad in the ribs because he turned

around to look at her and I said, What, dork, is it because she's Aryan? And he said, Chiiiill, woman.

At the time you couldn't figure out why that girl's beauty was enough to cause instant salivation and to make everything go slow motion in the schoolyard, as if she were walking around with her own soundtrack and projector and her own personal breeze blowing through her hair. It was because of the fucking theory of *persons* that not only vaunted bisexuality but also managed to convince you that a girl like the Arabesque or you yourself had to be more attractive than Marie-Amélie who okay might have been a hottie but she wasn't a nice person at all, no way.

But now you knew and your former naïveté made you laugh. You wondered how you could have believed in that theory for so long, when everything around you refuted it, anyone would think you had never switched on the television or looked at the photographs in magazines. Because honestly, who could aspire to anything if they didn't have Marie-Amélie's *body perfect*?

You could make a list: the weather girl on Canal + is sexually attractive, all the actresses and Madonna who's over fifty, even the actresses who play monsters are attractive and just camouflage it with fake body parts, the welcome hostesses at trade fairs, famous female singers and dancers at famous singers' concerts, models, the ugly women who get completely overhauled until they're sexy on those reality-television-surgery programs, the wives of presidents of the Republic when they curtsey to the Queen of England wearing a suit that matches their eyes, and then there are the sons of the presidents of the Republic who make the covers of the sleb press with headlines dripping like tears that say, "Sorry girls, he's taken," and that's not all, writers and pregnant ministers are so hot that the magazine *Marianne* asks them to talk about their first time just to get their summer readership even hotter, and frankly, mate, that Florian Zeller writer looks like he just walked off the set of one of those Timotei shampoo commercials, all the people who work in PR and fashion and television, and all the Spanish girls who get boob jobs for their eighteenth birthday, and the Lebanese girls who get nose jobs, and the Brazilian girls who get butt-lifts, and the other day at a family dinner your sister came in and told you that you can get your anus *whitened*, which means—because you already knew you could have hymen reconstruction and get your labia reduced—that the entire body right down to its most secret folds has become perfectible through surgery, can be offered up to ratification and correction as if all they're doing is fixing what was faulty to begin with—oh, right, sorry, that's where your cheekbone should have been, and your iris ought to have been that color and your mouth should have been plumper and your hair should be between 2 and 5 on the official chart of nuances, and always ever so carefully layered, and as for the construction site that is your body, it can be divided into several sectors, inside/outside, skin/hair, fat/bone, blood and sebum, all marked off with a dotted line, eagerly awaiting the needle that will bring the tightening thread and dying to meet its future architects, masons, and property developers, the ones who will redesign the arch of your eyebrows until even a Philippe Starck stool will pale in comparison, and they will feel you up in your most intimate places, right down to recolorizing your spinal cord, and then you will surrender completely to cosmetic surgery on the operating table, a living extension of the realm of the surgical knife.

On February 14, 2003, we were sitting in front of the television and enthusiastically applauding Dominique de Villepin. The Arabesque said, Seriously, tonight I don't even care that he's right-wing, and Mad said, He should have stood up and shouted, and I said, I hope Colin Powell is quaking in his boots, big time.

But it didn't change a thing, and in March, when the war really got going, we were still there the three of us cutting out our fliers and we couldn't help but prick up our ears, even though we knew that Iraq was way too far away: we had the vague impression that we could hear the planes flying over Baghdad and the bombs dropping.

But we couldn't hear anything. On we went, painstakingly cutting out our fliers, and we gave Mad a hard time because he wasn't cutting on the line and the bottom of the text got chopped off every time.

It was one of those evenings during the Great Inquisition of Love, an evening like so many others, when Mad and I emptied out two bottles of disgusting cheap red wine from the corner store downstairs, with me slumped on the sofa and him in the club armchair I'd dragged up from where someone had left it out on the street, and Mad turned to me and said, You know, I'm ashamed to say it, but I wanted to have it off with Marie-Amélie, too. I said, Yes, I know, no need to feel ashamed, dude. The entire planet wanted to have it off with Marie-Amélie, she was like Hélène de Fougerolles in *Le Péril jeune*, no more, no less.

Mad laughed: But I thought it was something serious, I thought you'd kill me if I talked about it, I got really stressed out about it and sometimes I thought I only wanted to screw her because I was sexually racist and she was the living allegory of *Keep Alabama White*. I shouted, What? And he said, There was something attractive about the way she represented everything we hated—the daughter of rich upper class white folk, with her straight blond hair, and her nail polish, and her Kookaï minidresses, remember? And I wondered if she didn't represent this sort of exotic place for me, you see, since I was black and not especially rich . . . It was torture, because I'd look at her 36C as usual (and you said, It was padded, dork, but Mad didn't hear) and I knew just what was going on, and then the next time I thought I just wanted to fuck this *white supremacy*, that I was no better than those white bitches who fantasized about black slaves on their cotton plantations, but my erotic exoticism was Paris and the sixteenth arrondissement, and Marie-Amélie's huge living room with the grand piano and the saber above the fireplace, shit man, you remember that living room?

No.

Of course you didn't remember that living room because you'd never set foot in it, and you could have reminded Mad just then that neither you nor the Arabesque had ever been invited and except for one night when you were so tanked that you wanted to go in and piss on her carpet—which you didn't do because you fell asleep at the Arabesque's place before you could get around to doing anything—you had always respected the Berlin Wall that separated her white capitalist apartment from your dark-skinned communist alleyways. And you could also have reminded Mad that whenever he went to see Marie-Amélie he went with Jérémie and his gang, and they left you two girls alone, thereby foiling any plans you might have had to hit on someone.

But instead I just sighed, Ah, shit, Marie-Amélie . . . And he said, Yes, I was a traitor . . . Me: And what about the theory of persons? Mad laughed: Did you believe it? I nodded. He said, You really are an idiot.

We had another drink and I thought about what Mad had said about being *sexually racist*. I wondered if it could apply to me—and I realized this just when I started discussing it with Mad—since I had always been attracted to guys who were foreigners or who could speak to me about foreign places, as if to be a blue-blooded Frenchman had to be a discriminatory failing. So according to the rules of the Grand Inquisition of Love, I told Mad about all the losers who had nothing going for them other than the fact that they weren't from here—the guy from Lebanon who wore a gold-plate pendant around his neck and whom I allowed to feel me up at school, even though I hated his little mustache and the gel he put in his hair; or the one I fell in love with because he was always talking to me about all the places he'd been, Yeah, babe, India is something else; or the guy who offered me a cigarette and told me I was as beautiful as a princess out of the Arabian Nights—And what made him a foreigner? interrupted Mad, and I said, He wasn't a foreigner, but who cares, the Arabian Nights, that's exotic. Like the guy in Egypt who said, *Arabic blood can feel Arabic blood*, and then all the others, too, the ones I didn't do anything with, but who attracted me all the same, just because of that.

While I was talking to Mad I couldn't help but think about the one who came from Algeria like me and how we watched the sun rise above the roofs of Paris at the end of another long night and who said, It's beautiful, and I said, Yes, it's beautiful like Algeria and Morocco and Syria, and he laughed, with his black eyes that were too small, and I kissed him as if this were the Promised Land, and so that I could embrace Algeria, and feel Algeria beneath my fingers, beneath my lips, and make love to Algeria, but I'd drunk too much. And I fell asleep curled up next to him thinking about dumbass things like dunes and hot sand and other erotic clichés about North Africa.

No exceptions to the theory?

Of course there were.

But what would be the point of telling Mad about S.? He was with you that year, the first or second one you spent in Paris, when you started your literature studies and you were living in that little apartment on the ground floor where you could look out and see *your* tree, and you had three cardboard boxes to store your books in, and one coffee cup; those were the days of your gang of friends who smoked mild tobacco and hated Sartre and boycotted Heidegger, who quoted Baudelaire with that bored air of people who experience the *spleen de Paris* firsthand every day and have nothing left to learn from it, and who tossed books on the floor that you grabbed by the cover between your thumb and index finger so you could look for that excerpt, no, not that one, turn the page, and you read, *That night, the great wheel of desire, so grave and wandering, perhaps visible to me alone . . . Will I ever shipwreck on another shore . . .* friends who lent you Neruda, initiated you into Joyce, laughed at your lack of skill in foreign languages, and read your short stories with that critical frown you came to dread, the ones who worked with you all night on that textual analysis on Apollinaire where women with green hair come to writhe beside the glasses of wine, and the ones who when they heard about a gang rape on the D line of the RER hinted discreetly that it was infinity placed within reach of penknives, and you would exchange complicit knowing glances before going on to deal with the possibility of ontological perfectibility.

Mad was back in France. It was my second year in Paris, by then; the first year he was still in Mali, stuck in Mali. In Paris he found a job with one of his cousins in a store by the Boulevard Raspail, where he shifted boxes, sold running shoes, and was bored. So every Friday night when I went out he would join us. For a whole year, every Friday night at nine at Saint-Michel, in his rainbow-colored jacket with his scent of rolling tobacco. Every time I'd get to the top of the métro steps there he'd be, leaning against the rust-covered barrier, and he'd toss his cigarette butt with a snap of his fingers and say, *Wassup,* giving me a tap on the back.

That's how he met S. at the same time I did, in one of our regular bars where we went to listen to music, and S. played tenor saxophone and always wore the same black shirt with a wing collar. S. had long hair that swept over his cheeks, and his gaze was blurry, and he had splendid hands that seemed to flutter right by my eyes since I obliged Mad to get us the table closest to the stage.

You were suffering from a real passion for saxophonists, it

was practically an obsession, you probably stole it from Marilyn Monroe, even though you would stubbornly deny it whenever Mad or the Arabesque made fun of you. You thought you'd heard somewhere that the sax was the instrument whose sound was closest to the human voice and even if you weren't sure about that, you knew that the way he played, with the instrument hugging the length of the musician's body, the way he held it close drove you crazy every time. And even now you can't help it, it's systematic, all it takes is for you to hear the strains of a sax as you come round a corner in a métro corridor for you to feel this pain in your guts and you absolutely have to see the musician, your eyes are burning, and you're sure he's got to be superb. You're often disappointed. But the fascination never wanes.

For a whole year I dragged Mad to the same café. With the sole purpose of seeing S. and hearing his sax. Every Friday evening, to look at him, smile at him, applaud his solo numbers, and I exhausted every possible variation in my wardrobe, and I'd try to dance when he played *The Autumn Leaves* so he'd see me on my feet, and I'd say, "Just one more smoke," whenever Mad was eager to leave, and I'd ask, "Will you be here next week?" and I realized there were a dozen of us playing the same game, and S. was oblivious to it all, or seemed to be anyway, and I'd listen to him talking to the other musicians and all his ideas were amazing. A whole year of fantasizing about the possibility that some day he would introduce not his next number but the fact that he was hopelessly in love with me . . . *and we lived together, the two of us, and I loved you, and you loved me.*

Somewhere along the line S. became my new cultural reference, and I couldn't help but think about what he would want me to do, and what he would dislike about me, so from then on S.'s imaginary gaze, like the eye in the poem, followed me everywhere—in the street, as I stood staring into my wardrobe, yes, even when I ate my cereal in the morning I would think about S. and sit up straighter and hum a little jazz tune.

A whole year and Mad didn't say a thing. When we took the métro together at the end of the evening, Mad had the tact to remain silent, and one time when I started crying he put his arm around my shoulder and went, *shhh, shhh* to calm me, and he shook me a little at the same time. And when suddenly S. gave me a kiss at the end of a set—probably because he'd had too much to drink, probably because some other guy was hanging around me, but I wanted so hard to believe that he *really* liked me—Mad was there to give me the thumbs-up and then a second later he was gone because he didn't want to be in the way.

Mad disappeared to let me live that night when S. took me to his place to show me the innovative musical instrument he'd invented: a dozen old-fashioned music boxes attached to a metal plate, that you played all at once. And I thought that God himself couldn't have found anything more original when, according to my grandmother, he invented the universe.

It was the night I discovered his giant poster of Chet Baker and three Schiele sketches on the wall of naked girls with orange nipples and blue-black hair. The next day I went out to buy the same ones.

It was the night S. said he wanted me, his breath acid with too much booze, and I thought you could not get more *sublime*, or even more romantic, than that.

It was the night S. laughed because I was wearing tights instead of stockings and garters. I would never know a more pathetic moment than that endless procession of seconds when he was trying to remove them and my tights—obviously—were clinging to my skin and the friction caused static electricity and in the darkness of his little room in Denfert-Rochereau we saw blue sparks fly up from the contact of his fingertips.

It was the night I nearly wept for joy because S. came into

me for the first time and everything he did was magical. So maybe I even convinced myself it was true when he asked me if I had come, and I said, Three times. And then I fell asleep curled up in a ball in the comforter that smelled of him.

But a few days later when S. stopped kissing me and informed me that he wasn't the sort of guy who was made for love and all that crap and I had better chill or grow up, because he hadn't signed up to anything with me, Mad was there again and Mad totally agreed never to set foot in that bar again where the concerts weren't all that great anyway and besides the beer had gone up fifty cents over the last six months, which was downright outrageous.

With hindsight, the fact that Mad had always been there was like an irrefutable proof. Apart from the years he spent in Mali, there was not a single event in your life that he had missed. He had always been there for you. So the promise you were going to make at the *mairie* to love him through sickness and health, for richer and for poorer, was nothing compared to the fact that Mad had been your friend in Normandy and in Paris, in a track suit or a tuxedo, drunk, hungover, there when you passed all your exams, when your love affairs went wrong, or publishers rejected you; he'd been there in the cold waiting for the night owl bus, in the heat of your vacation in Spain, in the ugliness of your homemade hairstyles and the beauty of your first push-up bra, through the night waiting for the sunrise, there in the train when the conductor threatened to make you pay a fine of 180 euros because you had graffitied your name, on his scooter, in the back seat of a taxi begging you not to throw up, there in the kitchen, in the bathroom, in poverty when you were counting out your last centimes to buy some pasta and in wealth during your first years at the École Normale Supérieure when you always paid for the champagne; Mad was there during the disasters, and the computer crashes, and the health problems, and the painful breakups where you had to drag a microwave halfway across Paris; Mad was there for your first publication, with a cigar and a bouquet of flowers, and for all the shows you'd been in since the lycée, Mad offered to beat up the 87 guys who'd made you unhappy, including the 62 who probably never even knew you existed—which meant Johnny Depp and the Hanson brothers, too—and he wiped your cheeks when they were sticky with mascara, and lent you his favorite sweater, and breathed down the back of your collar to warm you up, and held your hand, and never complained all the times you punched him in the stomach, and he massaged your feet after that horrible hike you went on in the mountains, and covered you with an extra comforter, and adjusted the pillow under your head. Mad had always always been there and he knew you better than anyone. If there was one couple on earth that was in with a chance, and finally, if there was one couple that could swear before the mayor without lying that they would endure until death, if there was one couple that could fearlessly undergo any interrogation in the Grand Inquisition of Love, it had to be you two.

But to get back to the Great History of Racism, before Iraq, before the fliers, there was April 21, 2002: you thought the last day had come for your threesome, and you were seized with panic inside. And you remember it as if it were yesterday. You can see the three of you in Mad's garage, early that evening.

April 21 was the Arabesque's birthday, and Mad and I were trying to find a present that was like her, which meant a present that would look as if it were dragging behind it all the history of the world, and we were trying to figure out how to build her a tandem bike. It's completely lame because she hasn't even got a guy, shouted Mad for the second or third time; the two of you are so inseparable you may as well be reps for some goodoo sect if you see what I mean. I see, shut up, I see and get that smile off your face, but then he went on, You're just like two first class dykes with Birkenstocks and the sleeves of your T-shirt rolled up on your shoulders, so don't be surprised if nobody dares try and come between you, you really think you can hit me, Alice, it's like those fans of Sapho's who get her autograph on the elastic of their Petit Bateau panties and every time the two of you show up at a party thinking you can hit on some guys, the guys wait for the precise moment when you go off alone together in a room so that they can take photos that they'll sell to *Muteen* for their next issue on lesbian fashion in nightclubs, and let me tell you, girl, let me tell you if you build a tandem for the Arabesque between now and tomorrow, everyone will ask why you put two bike seats instead of taking the opportunity to make it the first sex-toy vehicle in the history of intra-uterine eroticism, so I am not going to build some *fucking* tandem for two girls let me make that clear when half the lycée are already making jokes about bikes and dykes, no really have you never wondered why we get along so well the three of us without ever sleeping together even though we're a mixed threesome and mixed threesomes are always getting broken up because someone sleeps around—except for us, except for us because shit, you two are about as feminine as Frida Kahlo impaled by a girder, do I need to remind you where?—and I'm only telling you this for your own benefit because at our next party I'm going to look for Marlène and you can laugh, bitch, but in three or four days for sure I'm going to hit on her and *I'll give her fever* for hours while you and your Siamese twin on your tandem you'll be the Bayeux tapestry yet again but the lesbian version in a corner of the garden, and who's gonna have to take you back instead of staying with Marlène huh who else, me, and I always miss all my chances because of you Alice, because everyone knows no way can you keep your filthy mouth shut, always saying fuck every ten words and laying into any guy who might come up to you, because you allege—allege schmedge, you were just being your own guard dog, no, more like a guard jackal—that while you were talking they were ogling your tits instead of applauding your tirade about the latest joint you rolled or the lyrics to some song you've been playing on the keyboard for a month now in your super new band that I don't give a fuck about and no one gives a fuck about and that is why, Alice—

Mad—

Let me finish—no matter what you say, that's why you have not managed, not one single time—

The TV, man—

Not once, not one single time have you gone home without

me after a party—at Elisa's you pulled it on me, and at Lorène's, and Antoine's, and if it's not you it's the Arabesque crying over some loser and she needs my shoulder so she won't feel so alone, or so she'll feel more like a woman, it all depends, don't say it doesn't bug you on some level and—What about the TV?

You have before you now the mosaic of / the candidates' faces / and in a few seconds / from this mosaic / the faces of the two finalists / will emerge / it is eight o'clock / here is our assessment of the results of the first round of the presidential elections / An enormous surprise / Jean-Marie Le Pen has qualified for the second round with 17% of the ballot / Let me repeat that / the enormous surprise of this election.

It was the most horrible birthday we'd ever spent together. No one talked and everyone got drunk.

One beer after another. The Arabesque broke three glasses and glass was scattered all over the carpet of her living room but no one gave a fuck. That was when we started to believe that Mad would get sent back to Mali. More likely on a ship than on a plane in those days; it wasn't the fashion yet to use charters.

There was a girl who threw up in the bathtub fifteen minutes after she came in the door and the Arabesque asked me if I knew who she was. Mad asked me if I knew who she was. No one knew who this girl was and maybe she only came in so she could throw up and no one dared disturb her because it was somehow symbolic of the way we all felt. She spent the night in the bathroom curled up on the bath mat. I saw her the next morning when I was about to leave the Arabesque's place with a horrible hangover. She was smoking a cigarette in the bathtub and she said, Hi, sorry about yesterday. I told her no one gave a fuck. It was a crap birthday party.

All evening long we switched on the TV then switched it off again to see if the world was on fire, to see if people were demonstrating, or if the skinheads were celebrating, there was some talk of Molotov cocktails, of storming the Bastille again, we were saying fuck if he gets in I'll go into exile to organize the guerrilla movement. We wished we were in Paris, we talked about finding a car and leaving. People were sprawled here and there all over the living room and roughly every half hour someone shouted, It is A-fucking not possible, and then we'd switch off the TV again.

Off to one side Jérémie was saying, Shit, this is the first time I've ever voted in my life. We asked who he voted for and he went, Well, Noël Mamère, and someone said, You see, it's your fault, too, you shouldn't have voted for one of those marginal little candidates, obviously.[1] And Jérémie replied that that was not the issue, not at all. The issue was that this was the first time in his life he could vote, and now he would have to choose between Le Pen and Chirac in the second round, and just the thought of it was traumatizing him. Everyone was discussing, arguing, between a fascist and a crook, and everyone who couldn't vote said to Jérémie that however you looked at it the choice was easy. Unless you don't vote at all in the second round, said one girl with green ballpoint pen drawings on her forearms, and the Arabesque nearly tore her eyes out.

The booze was corroding my brain but not making me drunk, it was burning inside my head and eyelids and stomach, but I could not get drunk. I just slowed down and my eyes were practically gray they were so glassy, and Mad and the Arabesque and everyone around us, they too were glassy-eyed, exactly the same.

It was strange, that night, because for the first time you actually noticed a distinction between skin colors. Because when Mad got annoyed and started shouting at the Arabesque:

[1] In the 2002 elections Mamère ran for the Green Party. He obtained 5.25% of the vote. (T.N.)

Shut it, just shut the fuck up, you think it will change anything for you if he gets elected, with your good little girl face and looks, like some good girl uniform, you think they'll arrest you and send you home? Where the fuck would they send you, anyway, to the convent at Les Oiseaux? And the Arabesque's eyes misted up and her lips began to tremble, and you were looking at your hands and you could see how pale your skin was. You could see that you were a non-colored person too. Like all those little princesses with their snow white skin and blood hued lips and ebony black hair. Mad was the only person in the room who was black, the only one in the room who could not see blue veins through the skin on his wrist and who could not take a blue ID card from his wallet that would open all the doors. That night you realized that Mad didn't want to speak to you, that he knew, and you yourself knew, that it was just a game for you when you talked about your *bled*, or spoke Arabic; you knew that you were not African.

When Jérémie brought in the birthday cake Mad was still shouting and the Arabesque was crying. She suddenly got up and grabbed a slice of cake from her brother's hands and smashed it into her own face, saying, Are you happy now, Mad? What more do you want? I'm sorry I'm white, I'm sorry I'm French, does this make you happy? Look, I'm black, I'm black!

There was complete silence. Chocolate crumbs and icing were dripping from her face and her ear. Mad looked at her and didn't say anything. Jérémie began laughing quietly, then more and more loudly. Then Mad reached for another slice of cake and threw it at Jérémie, onto his fluorescent green T-shirt, right in the chest. I got a tiny piece of chocolate shaving in my eye and I shouted, Stop being such a jerk. And Jérémie, furious, took a slice of cake in turn and then everyone rushed over, shouting and laughing, screaming at Mad and the Arabesque, and the cake disappeared in a matter of seconds, smushed all over people's faces, and flung onto armchairs and into the mirror. The Arabesque didn't say a thing, just licked her lips, and then Mad went over and put his arms around her and she buried her head full of chocolate against his shoulder.

We instantly calmed down once the cake was finished. Jérémie dipped his finger into the slice crushed on the armrest next to him. Mad said, I'm sorry, I'm sorry, and the Arabesque was sobbing in his arms. I got up and went to join them with my tears.

That day, that evening of the Arabesque's seventeenth birthday, we really believed that civil war would break out, we thought the cops would be pounding on the door to come looking for any people of color to test them with some sort of special device for their colorimetry, and they'd shave the heads of girls who'd had sexual relations with those people of color, and they'd send the rest of them to get pregnant with blue-blooded Frenchmen according to some sort of fertility ticket distribution scheme in order to preserve the race; we believed that they'd be chartering long steel boats where they'd cram everyone into the hold and send them packing any old place to the four corners of the earth, we thought that Mad would have to leave, and Mommydaddy, and even Emilio Ramirez whom I hadn't thought about in years, and in this state of complete panic we almost believed it was the end of the world, that there would be no tomorrow, so we let red wine spill all over the carpet, and chocolate dribble down the mirror, and a strange girl vomit in the bathroom.

In this apocalyptic atmosphere Mad managed to attain one of his primary goals, since he slept with Marlène close by his side, because she wanted to protect him, and keep him there, because it might be the last time, and with tears in our eyes we really believed it, and we all hugged each other, and were fucking saying our solemn goodbyes, so by the time Le Pen was completely trounced in the second round we all felt a bit stupid.

—It was because of that party that you said yes?

That is what Mad asked me on the evening of the Arabesque's twenty-fourth birthday, and he was grinning from ear to ear and looking at the paper plate he was holding with a huge slice of Black Forest cake. I looked at him too and said, Don't even think about it. And then: *Maybe* it was because of that party.

Because Mad was the strongest, and everyone looked at him with admiration, because he would be the martyr that neither the Arabesque nor I could ever be, yeah I was almost envious of his situation, the danger he was in. What I meant was, Mad could join the Black Panthers if he wanted, he could raise his fist and lower his head, and it wouldn't be ridiculous. But could I—even with Mommydaddy's exotic half—could I ever be anything other than a little white princess pretending to be a *bougnoule?* I was jealous of Marlène, too, who could cling to him that night, who could enhance the pathos of the whole situation. Whereas I wasn't doing a thing, there was nothing I could do, so maybe, *maybe* when he suggested this marriage thing, it was my revenge, my way of experiencing commitment. I tried to explain it to Mad, starting over more than once, multiplying the, "well, you know what I mean"s and the "oh, I don't know"s. He winked at me and hummed, Yeah, yeah, *niggers wanna be me.*

I waved my finger at his slice of cake. He shouted, Hey, the Arabesque! then smashed the cake right into my face.

You can't remember just how much time you spent on it, in fact. You can't remember how many hours you wove your life stories together.

Did you really have to spend every Thursday night telling each other your experiences in detail for the sake of the Grand Inquisition? Now that you think back on it, it was more the fact that Mad and you got a sort of nervous pleasure out of it, an almost hysterical pleasure from wallowing in your confessions and secrets, throwing at each other's head the proof that you were not the passionless creatures you became in each other's presence. If you knew what that guy said to me when I took off my T-shirt, if you had seen that girl's eyes, if you had heard his cries, my sighs, him on top, me underneath, a little ecstasy, a little sweat, and our gazes full of provocation, as if they were shouting I beat you, just check my score before you start kicking up a fuss . . .

As the Thursdays went by, Mad and I seemed to be pouring ourselves out in sentences, tales, oceans of words, hours of explanations, and every question brought with it another unending track of phrases, and every expression imaginable came up because we started off with euphemisms like "do *it*" or "spend the night together," or we'd use a foreign language, I tended to go with English, Mad with Spanish, and the conversation was punctuated with things like "he went down on me" and "chupa" and then over time the euphemisms disappeared and we got right down to the rawness of the language, and all its variety, too, because French has so many expressions to talk about love and sex that you could spend all your Thursdays just counting them all.

One time Mad told me he had heard his buddies talk about their sex lives so much that he felt like he'd spent entire evenings playing sexual Clue. The person's name and the object changed, but it was always the same litany, with three elements, like, with Laetitia in the pantry on the washing machine, with Agathe in my room tied to the bed with a scarf, with Baptiste on the beach with suncream, with Laurent, with Colonel Mustard in the drawing room, with the rope, with Miss Scarlet, and I accuse Mr. Green, with What's-their-bucket, in such-and-such a place, like a nursery rhyme, and the list got longer and longer as the variations changed, but life in the end was nothing but a huge game of Clue.

You thought Mad was right, because like all teenagers you began by playing "Truth or Dare" and everyone knew that the whole point was either to get people to kiss each other, or to make them confess their latest prowess in this game of sexual Clue.

And then, once you were grown up, you played at *I never*, which was more or less the same thing, except that everyone had a beer in their hand and the game was like a challenge among the participants to find THE most original combination in order to dominate the others . . . On a cliff, a tractor-lawnmower, with a cosmonaut, in the baggage hold, at ten thousand meters of altitude—too easy—yes but ten thousand meters of altitude with a complete stranger, or two complete strangers, let's say three and leave it at that. Like everyone else you tried to come up with the most original experiences for your own life so you wouldn't have to drink, or so that you would—you never really understood the rules, so most of the time you sat quietly drinking your beer no matter what the variations on the sexual Clue were, and you looked admiringly at the girl at the edge of the circle who was drinking—or not drinking?—with each assertion she made, because she'd done it all, absolutely everything, maybe even with a cosmonaut on a bearskin in the hold of the *Queen Mary.*

One evening I played with Mad and the Arabesque, it was during a fairly pathetic party, at a friend of a friend's from the lycée. There were a dozen or so of us sitting in a circle, including Jérémie who was on the opposite side of the circle and to whom I was trying to send sidelong gazes full of unmistakable meaning but *not* insistent. I was wearing, on purpose, a pair of panties that matched my bra for once, because I believed the Arabesque when she said that what mattered was not making yourself beautiful—because I would just look like some ordinary slut—but to feel beautiful and feel ready. So in addition to my underwear I was wearing my usual beige corduroy jeans and a brown T-shirt, no make-up, my Converse sneakers and a pair of earrings that the Arabesque had made for me out of Fimo, and which were cracking.

I remember that party really well because it was in the days when I really dreaded playing that game, where I could only confess that I had never done *anything.* The Arabesque was no further along than I was and that braggart Mad who always went around telling everyone he'd had his first sexual relations at thirteen had promised not to trap us and not to choose sentences that would oblige us to reveal the shameful truth or to lie—which was absolutely contrary to the spirit of the game.

Mad had a girl in his arms, and you seem to recall it was Marlène, but it couldn't have been, because they only hooked up later, much later, and this game was right at the beginning of the lycée, whereas the Mad and Marlène thing only started at that epic birthday party on April 21, so it was some girl you don't remember but let's say it was Marlène because it doesn't matter anyway, and in any case they ended up holding each other like that, Mad and her, clinging together in a way that was every bit as obscene, tangling themselves together like ivy and trunk, even if it would only be the following year.

What you remember, above all, the reason why that party has stayed with you—and why you may never forget it—is that for the first time you realized you were in the process of becoming a *sexual* creature.

You couldn't feel it physically, but it came through the transformation of language. Because words that up to then had always made you giggle, and which in the end were only interesting as extensions of words-you-must-never-say, as transgressions of Mommydaddy's rules, were suddenly filled with meaning, and the reality they represented made you feel horribly ill at ease.

That night it was as if I were losing an entire chunk of my vocabulary, as if it were slipping away from me. All the words I had always used without any problem up until then, even with a certain pleasure—the pleasure of knowing that I was being crude, and that Mommydaddy would not allow that word at the dinner table—were suddenly putting up a resistance. They became inseparable from a shameful blush or an awkward stammer. Ironically, it was at the very moment when you needed those words most—because you were discovering the reality behind the words—that they refused to be tamed, or even used. As if those words you had laughed about so often— now it was their turn to giggle.

You couldn't say them, you couldn't write them. You forced yourself, though, for a few years you tried to write them in your diary, or in your stories, but even the word "skin," or the word "kiss," was enough to bring your pen to a halt, and you would wait above the sheet of paper, speaking out loud, practically insulting yourself for being incapable of talking about these things. Fuck, do it Alice, go ahead, write it down. But even in the solitude of your room you would blush, oh yes, this stinging embarrassment rising from your throat all the way to your ears, and it was impossible. That evening, between Mad and his slut, not to mention the Arabesque who was guzzling Bailey's, you lost some of your language.

From that moment on, you became all the more sensitive to those words when other people wrote them as well, as if it were a proof of your own block.

And yet it wasn't the first time you'd ever seen them: ever since you were little you would steal books from Mommy-daddy's bookshelf and devour whatever you happened upon without bothering to submit the text to parental censorship. You remember how you saw "bastard," and "lick," and "orgasm," and in Philip K. Dick there was the woman who broke the man's neck and, *by the way,* she was holding his head between her legs.

Until that day those words may have been incomprehensible, but they never seemed to draw attention to themselves on the page. Suddenly now when I read them I had a strange impression, as if I were seeing someone I'd lost track of long ago in the background in some news footage, or in a commercial at the movie theatre. In Faulkner the *dirty little sluts* were scoffing at me, and then—shit, this passage is really terrible—the bloody ear of corn, and then there was Anaïs Nin, and D.H. Lawrence of course, *head slightly bent but heart full of hope,* even in Boris Vian, my refuge, the great love of my years at the lycée, the words would hide then greet me derisively when doors slammed *with a sound like a slap on a naked buttock.*

You would have to wait a few years—five? six?— for that whole realm of vocabulary to allow itself to be tamed once again, so that you could set yourself free from this partial aphasia. You would have to wait for Théo's room and all the years spent preparing for your university exams, where patiently, page by page, your reading would lead you on a veritable pilgrimage back to the lost words. Yes, with great patience, by dint of quotations and discussion, and invoking the tutelary powers of Laclos and Rimbaud and Genet, and murmuring in alcoves and boudoirs, and whispering punctuated with laughter, Théo would restore those words of love and vice, and you would be able, if not to write them—it's still a problem, even today—at least to say them, without stumbling over them and turning bright red.

So that night, the night of playing *I never,* I understood that something had changed in me, without warning, and stirred by a strange warmth it seemed to go straight from my belly to my words, now trapped behind the barrier of my teeth, the screen of my burning cheeks, and at that very moment everything became clear: why I felt ill at ease when I heard Gainsbourg's voice, or when Errol Flynn kissed Maid Marion at the window of her chamber and behind her you could see *the bed,* and why the bass in rock songs vibrated longer inside than it used to, and why I would nervously press my knees together whenever Jérémie was talking to me, and why I hated Beckett when he spoke of the open bunghole in a woman's middle, and why I spent hours tenaciously studying the outline of my naked body in the big bathroom mirror while my sister was banging on the door and shouting, Move your ass, I cannot believe it, I want to brush my teeth *now!*

So I looked anxiously at Mad, hoping that this transformation hadn't affected him as well, that I wouldn't suddenly discover that he too had taken on a new meaning. But Mad was the same as ever, and I didn't think he was either handsome or ugly, I didn't want to touch his skin or kiss his lips, and although he was persistently piling on circumstantial details in hopes of winning the game of *I never,* his words rang clearly, they were transparent, you could make your way through them. They weren't like other sexual words, which for me seemed to hide troubled waters, as if shrouded in smoke, they even seemed to have a certain smell, probably because of that party, words like "sleep with" and "fuck" and "fellatio" and "cunnilingus": they smelled like hashish. Exactly like that Afghan hashish Jérémie used to shape into very fine serpentines and place on the rolling paper in the hollow of his hand.

Mad and I began to gather the necessary documents to go and file our application at the *mairie*. Birth certificates, proof of residence, IDs, and then the medical exam, which made no sense to me. As if I had to make sure the toy I was giving to Mad was not broken—pink lungs, a sturdy heart, deep red blood, bones with the right dose of calcium, and on his side white teeth, elastic skin, firm muscles and a straight spine.

—Your woman is healthy, I said to him when I came back to the apartment, and he was radiant because he had finally received his birth certificate, which he had had to ask his aunt in Mali to get for him; he had waited so long and now finally it had arrived.

—Victory, he shouted, with a big grin, and he was on his feet, immense, in my tiny little home, his tall self stretching from floor to ceiling.

I threw my arms around him, and he held the document above his head for fear I might crease it.

We added it to our file in the blue paper sleeve. Mad smoothed it with his hand, almost religiously, and smoothed all the other pages too. It was as if he were making a cradle, or an altar, or some mixture of the two, a crèche.

You didn't even have the heart to make fun of him because it was an important moment. You were nearing your goal. You could tell.

We had nearly everything we needed for our blue file. Even

though Mad's residence permit was only temporary, according to the law that could not stop the mayor from celebrating the marriage. The law simply stated that the mayor would systematically refer the case to the public prosecutor, and the prosecutor would decide whether to call for an investigation and perhaps delay the wedding. But we were ready for our encounter with Edvige. We almost hoped it would come as soon as possible so that we could triumph once and for all over the tentacular monster.

Mad now knew that I was a cornflakes addict, and that my favorite color, we'd decided, was red, and that we'd have two kids, a boy and a girl, and I'd like them to be twins but Mad didn't care and we'd call them Héloïse and Alexandre. So Edvige had better behave, because at the quiz for the ideal couple, no one can touch our crew, that is for sure.

—What do we still need? I asked.

Mad looked up from the file with a half smile.

—Other than the ring on your finger?

—If you give me one, make sure I can wear it on my middle finger.

He ruffled my hair with his fist and called me a mean kid, and I shouted like when I was ten, "Truce!" and "That hurt!" When he let go of me I asked him why he had brought up the ring when he didn't even have the means to buy me a drink at the bar downstairs. I told him to stop boasting. He made as if to grab me again and I rushed to the far side of the table, still laughing and panting.

—Already if you buy me even one beer, our nuptial beer, that would be great. Or, know what? A pair of sneakers? Can you nick one at Raspail? Really cool golden ones, okay? Please my darling give me some golden wedding sneakers . . .

And Mad said, We can open a registry at Nike!

And I said, Yeah! And at Lacoste!

—We can ask for baseball caps!

—And name bracelets.

—And shiny hair gel!

—And multicolored elastics for your little braids!

We were laughing so hard we collapsed on the sofa.

After ten minutes of silence then sudden laughing fits, which gave us time to find a few more silly gift ideas, Mad said we each had to choose a witness. We both said, "easy" at the same time. And looked at each other at the same time and said, in the same voice, "the Arabesque."

—Oh no, shit!

We fought over her, about who was closer to her, and why do you always have to do like me? Mad suggested gambling for her at poker. I protested vehemently in the name of ethics. He offered to do the dishwashing for a whole year if I'd let him have her, and I said, The Arabesque is *inalienable*.

—If we're already fighting over who gets custody of our friends before the wedding, said Mad, what's it going to be like when it's time to divorce?

—If we start thinking about divorce already . . .

But I fell silent because it was a *mariage blanc*, after all. And marriages of this nature had a specific shelf life. Best before the date on the lid, as Papa said to me. A marriage with an expiration date four years down the road.

And then, the divorce, and we'd have to start another file in a blue paper sleeve. I told Mad that at the medical exam we should have asked for a health check for just four years. Because we might have to go through a new technical check for the divorce. To make sure our throats are constricted, and our tear ducts are in working order, and our hearts are broken.

He put his arm around my shoulder and shook me gently and said everything would be fine, yes, everything would be fine, he would be a perfect husband and a model divorcé. And he even let me have the Arabesque, in the name of the female complicity that has always united us, whereas for him, no way, clothes swapping and frenetic shopping expeditions to Petit Bateau, not his scene at all, so you keep the Arabesque, and when we divorce I'll leave her to you, too, I won't cut anything or anyone in half just to keep my share, not even that dumb down pillow that I could certainly claim I have a right to. You see, aren't I kind and conciliatory, besides I can ask someone else to be my witness, say Jérémie, for example.

I started to laugh: Isn't that kind of strange—Jérémie? And Mad said, No, no, it'll be perfect.

Yes, it will be perfect, teamwork right to the end.

And at its core the quartet created by two childhood friends, overlapping with a trio from the lycée, and a brother-sister duet, and the teenage love story that bound me to Jérémie, he even kissed me once, during a party at the Arabesque's place, he was just walking by to get a drink before going off to another party and I was out on the terrace with Mad and Mad went back in to get a drink so Jérémie said, You want some smoke? And I said, *Yeah, sure.*

So we stayed out there sitting on the wooden deck, smoking, lit by the anti-mosquito lamps placed at each corner of the terrace and Jérémie said that the light was flattering, dancing over me, and I immediately felt this nerve above my lip threaten to start trembling and he asked if there was anything between Mad and me and I said no, then was there anything between Mad and his sister, and I said no again. *And the more you say no to Jérémie, the more you feel like you're shouting just the opposite, that your body is twisted in a strange position—to show off your breasts and hide your profile—and you're biting your lips and blocking your laughter as if you were already accepting some proposal he hasn't even made yet, and won't make. If Jérémie knew the first thing about body language, he would read I do yes I do on every curve and every angle you are offering, bending, retracting, I do yes I do, please, until death do us part,* and he laughed and asked me didn't we get a little bored. Then his buddies' car stopped just outside the house and they beeped the horn, so Jérémie leapt to his feet and said, Gotta go. But he'd left his backpack right by me and when he leaned down to pick it up he kissed me. *You feel the acidity of his rolling tobacco on his lips, the brown juice that almost stings and the quick caress of his tongue, not in your mouth, just grazing your lips, and you get the strange impression that you are liquefying, spilling out of yourself, in water and heat between your legs, that you're flowing away until you might disappear altogether.* But he left at once, with a laugh, before I had time to find out what might happen, and he jumped in the car and you could hear the radio blaring some bad metal, too loud. I went back into the living room and collapsed into an armchair. Mad raised an eyebrow but didn't say anything.

Jérémie didn't come back all night and I waited but I didn't want to tell the Arabesque why, and I sat drinking tea, repeatedly, waiting for him to come back, but that night he went out with one of Eva's girlfriends and there were never again any occurrences of that nature.

Since that night I have had a particular fondness for the Arabesque's terrace.

Our quartet is so indissoluble that the icy hands of Edvige will find no faults through which to slip. And *the state prosecutor is entitled to conduct any investigations that might be deemed useful.*

You like to tell yourself, in secret, that it's not only Mad, it's also the Arabesque, in a way, and above all Jérémie, in a way, whom you are going to marry in the *mairie* of the tenth arrondissement, because in spite of the passing of time, and all the successful kisses that have relegated that clumsy kiss on the terrace to the rank of Little Mermaid eroticism, you can't quite forget that night after all, you with your huge mug of tea that never seemed to empty, sitting on the rug in the Arabesque's living room, you were dreaming that Jérémie would ask you to marry him, or that he would rush through with a bunch of gangsters hot on his heels and just before he threw himself out the bay window he'd find the time to say, Quick, Alice, we gotta go, they're after me but I came back for you, I couldn't leave without you . . .

Or maybe the guy next to you might get too sticky as the evening progressed and, sigh, might try to force a kiss on you, shoving you up against the wall, with a horrible laugh, and then Jérémie would come for you again—but he'd spare the bay window this time, or maybe not, because you liked the idea of all that broken glass—and he'd punch the guy right in the jaw and make him crumple to the floor. And then Jérémie would say something like, No one has the right to touch Alice, and then he'd apologize for having gone off earlier and he'd say that he'd needed time to think and that he'd never felt that way before, I love everything you do you are so you are so, *marry me*.

Except in the file in the blue sleeve, there's Mad's name. Because Mad is the one who popped the question and I said *I do yes I do*.

Sometimes you wonder, if you had met your Prince Charming before, would Mad have asked someone else to marry him? Maybe the Arabesque? And then you and Jérémie would have been the witnesses. And this whole business about a *mariage blanc* would have made you laugh, *vive la liberté*, that was one on Brice Hortefeux, and standing there ever so quietly at the bottom of the steps, to Mad you would say, *High five man*, and to the Arabesque, *Respect*.

But obviously that's all academic today.

One summer during the lycée years, a summer like any other, when I'd dragged Mad and the Arabesque to Mommydaddy's seaside holiday house, one of the first summers the Arabesque had her driver's license and was forever shouting, Let me concentrate, fuck, I'll go off the road, that summer the three of us underwent a major trial in the Great History of Racism.

One evening we were on the pier drinking cans of 8.8 and smoking some rolled cigarettes that kept going out because of the wind. It was one of those awesome evenings when the most absurd discussions turned passionate and you could see the spark in the Arabesque's big blue eyes that meant this was really a special time. Her eyes always work like a barometer and you can tell if the party's a success just by looking at her. When there's no spark there, when nothing manages to light her eyes, the party will never be anything more than just okay, that's how it is.

We were watching the sun go down on the ocean, just like I'd done hundreds of times since I was little. On the opposite side, a few meters from the pier, there were guys on the square with cooler boxes full of beers, and we would go and replenish our supplies from time to time, trying to come up with funny things to say to get a discount, and when the Arabesque was sufficiently drunk she went over in her bathing suit, in spite of the cold wind that had started blowing, and she came back with an armful of cans, shouting, "Victory!" Mad lifted two fingers nonchalantly above his shoulder without even turning around, and I'd reached the point where I thought both of them were dead magnificent and I launched into a great declaration of love that got a bit muddled.

By around midnight it was really very cold. The Arabesque said her hair was sticky with salt from the spray. We considered leaving, but we were in no great hurry, lying on the sand that was starting to get cold underneath, too, so we might have said it a few times. It was just a good feeling knowing there was no reason to hurry, that we'd have the house all to ourselves whatever happened, and that we had the whole week ahead of us to laze around like that.

It was that sort of impression that summed up the happiness of those lycée years, an impression of intense pleasure, a feeling of being all-powerful. As if you could see poetry wherever you turned, in the smallest things, even when Mad spat his beer out because it had gone down the wrong way and there were drops glittering in the light of the streetlamp on the square. Because you were sixteen years old and you saw beauty everywhere, in your scribblings in art class or the way Mad massacred *Stairway to Heaven* on his guitar. Everywhere.

—Okay, this time I'm out of here, said the Arabesque after half an hour had gone by, and she got up and started picking up the cigarette butts on the ground around her.

I sat up with a grunt, slow and lazy, and Mad leapt to his feet, just to show off. We headed for the house with our arms around each other's shoulders, singing *Dans le port d'Amsterdam* even more off key than usual.

When we'd left the town behind and were on the little road that goes along the dunes, we saw a group of guys drinking in a field next to a trailer. Since Mad was lagging behind us, trying to climb a tree a few yards from there, the guys went, Yoo hoo girls, waving their arms, and we said, Good evening.

—Have you got any cigarette paper? they asked.

The Arabesque replied, Sure, always, so we went over to the fence to toss the packet to them and we made a few remarks about their barbecue and it looked like they were having a good time. They said why not come and have a drink with them, the fire would keep us warm in spite of the wind, we called out to Mad who was roughly halfway up his tree and we told him we were climbing over the fence and we were just there on his left. And he should come and join us when he'd had his fill of acting the idiot.

—I'll just plant my flag on the summit then I'm coming.

The Arabesque had already sat down on a little camping chair and around us there were five guys all in their twenties and one girl with a little baby in a basket right there next to her. They all had the local accent, a really horrible accent where every vowel sounds like it's an "o." One of the guys handed me a glass with a meaningful smile. He was bare-chested, standing over the barbecue, and his arms were absolutely splendid—I was in my *arm* period in those days, which came immediately after my *hand* period, and the Arabesque was in her *green eyes, definitely* period, and he said, Hey, I'm Simon. We talked about vacation, things like have you been coming here for long? And whose is the baby? And the trailer? Simon sat next to me and the Arabesque also found herself an attentive escort who was wearing this hideous cap, and we looked at each other from our folding chairs, raising our eyebrows now and again and laughing, delighting already in how Mad would react when he came and saw how wrong he always was about our charm potential, because frankly we were the sort of girls who could inspire guys to fall to their knees and say, I've been madly in love with you from the start and I adore everything you do and I didn't dare say anything until now but *marry me*. And Mad was just being a cretin.

He finally showed up, rubbing his knees and removing the dried pine needles that were clinging to his sweater.

When Simon asked, Is he your friend? I didn't notice the change of mood around us and I just answered with a big smile, Yes he is, and not just any friend, we've known each other all our lives. The guy gave this little honking laugh between his teeth and before I could even ask him what his problem was—because you were beginning to realize there was a problem, idiot, but you were still a long way from guessing which one—one of the other guys said to Mad, Have you come for your friends? If you don't mind, we'll hang on to them for a little while.

And Simon said, Yeah, and even if you do mind.

I saw the Arabesque, who had been leaning over the baby basket, suddenly lift her head, and in the light of the barbecue you could see her face was red and shining. Mad didn't know how to take the remark so he tried to laugh it off, but it didn't work. With his hesitant smile he asked, You think they're all that nice?

—Too nice for you anyway.

I got up and went over to Simon to say, Just what is going on? But he merely stretched out his arm and blocked my path with an expression as if to say, *Mind your own business,* and the girl with the baby, who must have witnessed scenes like this a dozen times already, came up behind me and told me not to be afraid.

Because they weren't going to hurt Mad, not much, they were just going to teach him a lesson. Teach him that he mustn't go around stealing French women. And it would serve as a lesson to the Arabesque and me, too. Because we mustn't go hanging around with blacks. Let alone fuck them. Because all they wanted was to take advantage of us and get money from the government. And manufacture dozens of kids who'd work so that they wouldn't have to.

She even put a consoling hand on my shoulder and said, You know, me too, when I was younger I made that kind of mistake, I was attracted to them. They must have some sort of secret, something like magic, or voodoo, that attracts white girls. They must have made a pact with Satan.

—You are sick in the head, I said.

—Yeah, I may be a bit drunk, but you know what I mean, huh, you get it, don't you? That's the idea, that's the whole point. You mustn't ever sleep with blacks.

In the meantime the Arabesque had gotten to her feet, too, but the guy next to her was holding her by the wrist. She shouted at him to let her go and he said, What, you like that guy or something? And he added some insane rubbish about blacks and big dicks and the Arabesque being a slut.

Mad had his back against the trailer and was moving slowly away from the group, hugging the trailer as if he had forgotten how to run.

—You afraid or something? said Simon.

—Asshole, said Mad.

Simon grabbed one of the chairs and threw it at him. It hit Mad in the shoulder. After that everything went very quickly.

I shouted, Let's get out of here! The Arabesque dug her nails into the hand of the guy who was holding her and said, Fuck, let me go, fucking bastard, and for a moment I was tempted, I guess from seeing too many bad movies, to kick over their barbecue and bury one or two of the guys under the burning charcoal. But the Arabesque got free and the guy wasn't really in earnest, it was enough for him to know he'd made her panic completely for a minute there. Mad was the first one to start running, as if in slow motion to begin with, then hitting his normal stride, and behind us one of the guys took a handful of wooden kebab skewers and threw them at us, then beer bottles, and he shouted, *Fuck, to think I wasted good money on booze for women who suck blacks,* it may even have been Simon shouting, then another one said, *Don't ever come back here or we'll bleed you dry,* and the blonde said in a really strange, shrieking voice, *Be careful girls, make sure you don't get tricked, or touched,* and all three of us were running like crazy, and someone else shouted, *My father committed suicide because of those Africans who stole his job*, and we were still running, *He probably has AIDS, you'll get infected,* and then when they stopped shouting they began laughing, this jolly, pleased sort of laughter, oh wasn't that a good one, and I shouted, *You wasted your good money on an Algerian woman, asshole,* and the Arabesque said, Oh shut up, Alice, save your pride for later. We must have kept running for half an hour or more, all the way to the house, and we locked ourselves in, slamming home the bolts and closing the shutters, and we laid out the kitchen knives in the middle of the table until at last we calmed down.

—I forgot my sweater back there, said the Arabesque, at least ten times.

And Mad, over and over, I almost got lynched, I almost got skewered, I would have ended up on their fucking barbecue, fuck, who were those people? Finally the Arabesque wondered if we should call the police.

—For racial intimidation?

—They'll only say we were trespassing.

—We'd been drinking.

—And smoking.

—They won't do anything, the scum.

With hindsight, you think that you should have tried, done something, no matter what, and not just left them there, smug and triumphant, casually putting a second batch of sausages on the barbecue and raising a toast to your terrified faces. But at the time all you could think of was holding each other close and not seeing anyone. Because that night was maybe the last station of the Great History and you felt as if you'd had a close call with death.

—If they'd caught us, said the Arabesque several times over, each time embellishing the various forms of torture and abuse she imagined, with bizarre details, who knows what they might have done to us . . .

By the end of the evening the story of her escape sounded like something Houdini could have done, and she asserted that the moment she set foot on their territory she could tell those guys were sketchy, and you could almost imagine them with three heads and reptilian tongues they wiggled in a really obscene way, and their laughter was like Batman's enemy's, and they must have a stockpile of weapons of all sorts hidden under their trailer.

We went up to bed. The Arabesque and I were sharing the big bed in my parents' room —because it was *sooo* soft and comfy—and Mad was in the kids' room with the bunk beds. Just as we had nestled into the sheets he came in dragging his mattress behind him and asked if we didn't mind if he slept in there with us.

In the end we put all the mattresses on the floor and slept all three of us on an immense expanse of comforters and pillows. We snuggled up together with Mad in the middle and the Arabesque, her voice faint and full of sleep, said one last time, Still, that was a close call.

—I would have protected you, I said, over Mad's shoulder.

He protested vigorously: I'm the one who would have protected *you*, girls, I'm the guy.

—But you were the main victim, said the Arabesque.

Mad sighed and I told him that he ought to take up boxing.

—If you go on pissing me off, I'll give you AIDS.

I burst out laughing. The Arabesque immediately shouted that it wasn't funny, but she laughed a little anyway, and Mad made it worse by saying, Or I'll do some voodoo on you, yeah, that's what I'll do, that's where blacks are super-powerful, voodoo and our sense of rhythm, bro, I'll do some voodoo while I dance the be-bop, mam'selle, and what're you gonna do to stop me? So I chimed in and said that I'd do my *flying car-*

pet act on every single one of them, flying carpet with loads of spices in the couscous, and the Arabesque sat up in bed and gave us the finger, shouting that she would *camembert* and *vinify* the hell out of us.

We finally fell asleep, smiles on our faces.

Because you were sixteen years old and the Great History of Racism didn't scare you. Because you were the deadliest trio of all time. Once again you had defeated the army of Evil, and all you'd left behind was one sweater. And you still had a whole week of vacation ahead of you.

I would have the Arabesque as my witness, and Mad would have Jérémie. This list with two names on it completed our marriage file. Now we had to go and submit it and, at the same time, set the date, and Mad had read the texts about all this—publish the banns.

This formality seemed really odd because it sounded like something straight out of a novel by Alexandre Dumas or even Robin Hood, and you were obsessed by it. For you, publishing the banns was when someone with knee breeches and a feathered hat went around pasting handwritten notices on the walls of thatched cottages or sent them with arrows into the stones of a château wall, where they would suddenly unfurl in a gesture of derision against all the bad guys lurking around.

You had trouble seeing how you and Mad could go about publishing your banns in such a thrilling way. Unless, of course—daydreaming over your morning coffee—you sent them flying through an open window straight into the offices of the Ministry of Immigration and National Identity, where the arrows would land with a muffled little *thock* in the velvety tapestries in the wall, and then, on the verge of an apoplectic fit, livid with a seething rage, every Edvige in the Ministry would learn of your marriage with Mad and run to the window to see who had had the nerve to . . .

Outside, her bow on her shoulder, and dressed just like Will Scarlet, the Arabesque would thumb her nose at them then jump onto Jérémie's skateboard. The two of them would vanish into the distance, zigzagging among the cars, and the Minister would set a price on their heads and say, I want them dead or alive. The veins on his forehead would swell. His voice would drop a full octave. With his finger on a secret button he would summon his fearful guard of mysterious creatures . . .

But Mad explained to me that the requirement to publish banns was anything but heroic and didn't call for any quivers.

The future marriage had to be made public so that before the ceremony anyone who saw a reasonable motive to oppose it could come forward and say so. The moment Mad told you this, you thought back to that traumatizing scene in so many films where the thundering voice of the mayor or the priest orders: If any person can show just cause why they may not be joined together, *let them speak now or forever hold their peace.* The formula is magnificent and terrifying, and for a few seconds, the silence too.

You could not help but wonder what would happen if you spoke or if someone really did have a just cause to make known. All the danger threatening the future married couple would be concentrated in that moment, a few seconds of waiting, and for you and Mad it could be the Arabesque, or Jérémie—what if he had been madly in love with you ever since that night on the terrace?—shouting that your marriage was a sham, or Mommydaddy might suddenly show up and tell you they'd changed their mind. The mayor would freeze and say, I've known right from the start, how did you think you could get away with it? And then stupor, and shock, and shouts, and the president's portrait on the wall would come alive to strike you dead on the spot, or the police might come storming in, and Edvige would be victorious and walk on your corpses.

Let them speak now or forever hold their peace . . . As if everything hinged on those few seconds, and then the bubble of marriage would close again around man and wife protectively. From then on tongues could wag their evil gossip all they liked, man and wife would hear none of it, no piece of gossip could ever harm them, not even the ugliest adultery, filthiest incest, revelations of crimes of passion, disturbing fetishism, no, nothing ever again, because the ceremony had decreed that all of that would be *held forever*, buried for good in the bowels of the earth.

But that only held true for real weddings.

In the case of the one I would be contracting with Mad, it was of the utmost importance to implore the guests to hold their peace now *and* forever.

That was probably what was hardest for me about the whole procedure: not the Inquisition, or the state prosecutor, or the little girl's dreams I must forget about, but the lie, day in, day out.

Because both of you knew that everyone could feel trapped by the order to speak now or forever hold their peace. How could you be sure of people, even your friends, even those with whom you hoped to share your victory over Edvige? There were thousands of reasons to oppose what you and Mad planned to do . . . Just think. There were people who didn't give a damn about politics, and people who didn't see things the way you did; there were people who invested so much hope in a white dress, and others who might sincerely love their foreign fiancé, and now they would be placed under suspicion precisely because of phony couples like you and Mad; and then there were those who were afraid of getting caught up in something illegal, those who simply loved the truth . . .

So when Mad and I began talking about the banns and publicizing our marriage, it soon became obvious that we couldn't make up a list of reliable, or even unreliable people, we couldn't sort through our friends to decide who could be in on it and who couldn't. For a start, we were afraid. So we said, Let's not tell anyone. Because we couldn't risk people finding out it was a *mariage blanc* and then blabbing about it, not now that we'd established my favorite color was red and Mad was in on my favorite brand of cereals.

After fear came sadness, when I told Mad that we could not insult our friends by inviting them to a masquerade, either, by asking them to attend something they would assume was a real wedding, and we came to realize that we'd be all alone, just our usual quartet—Mad, myself, the Arabesque and Jérémie, because Mommydaddy had told us they would rather not attend.

—This really will make it look like a *mariage blanc*, said Mad.

But I couldn't force Mommydaddy to come and lie for my sake.

After a while I told Mad that my sisters were in on it and that maybe they would agree to come and we might feel a little better if there were six of us. They accepted without hesitation and when I heard my little sister's shriek of delight I wondered if she had ever recovered from the crush she had on Mad when she was five years old and he was eight and he was teaching her how to read.

And now here they are on our wedding day, and my big sister was almost late and she's all flustered and on getting out of the car she says to Mad, straight up, You look a total pimp in that suit, frankly you ought to be ashamed. And it feels good to have them here.

But you didn't tell anyone else, or else you lied, and it has been a heavy burden, day after day. Even if all of you, including the Arabesque and Jérémie, agreed that it was better this way, you won't always be able to stick to this line of conduct without feeling some disgust, no way. It simply isn't possible.

There was the time when we were on our way to the *mairie* to drop off our file and we ran into Théo, Théo whom I haven't seen since I was preparing my exams. I know he would never object to what we are doing because we talked about politics a lot. But I grabbed Mad by the arm and we swore to each other that even if we trusted someone we would not start spreading the news or the truth behind the news. So when Théo asked what we were doing there, we mumbled something and Mad said voter registration yadda yadda, casting a worried glance over to the main entrance to make sure Edvige wasn't standing there listening to us. Théo smiled at me, somewhat taken aback. And I thought that maybe I should tell him, just because we looked so suspicious, Mad and I, with our papers in our hands.

But since you were the one who had played the high priestess of free love with Théo, sexual and sentimental, you couldn't go getting married at your age, and he might suspect something was up if you said marriage, and you wanted him to suspect something was up, because it was unbearable to think Théo might believe you were about to settle down and sacrifice yourself on the altar of marriage when you had spat upon it so often in the past.

What you really wanted was to shout out loud—against yourself, against Mad, against people—and proclaim the truth, forever, and take the entire street as your witness.

I would have liked to say to Théo, Come to the wedding, because it's an act of political rebellion, and afterwards we can get drunk on red wine and talk about Proudhon the way we used to—but I couldn't. Nor could I say to him—because he has nothing good to say about marriage or coupledom—nor could I say to him, Come to a real wedding, a celebration of love, we're keeping it simple, just a few friends. So I said, The elections, this is my arrondissement, and I wondered how believable I sounded.

Théo went on his way, with a shout that I should call him, we should go and have a drink together sometime that week. I said *I do yes I do* but what I was thinking was, four years from now, more like. When I'll be free from the lie.

Just then, running into Théo like that, I felt like puking; I was bent double with disgust. And the feeling kept coming back, in waves. Always with this desire to stop everything, to toss all the papers into a dumpster, even the list of Mad's good deeds that I kept enumerating to remind myself why I have to help him. Sometimes I was really on the verge of calling the whole thing off. It seemed so pointless, it seemed as if it would never end. At any time someone could go and denounce a *mariage blanc . . .*

So I thought, lying like this for four years, until he gets his nationality, and then can you divorce, finally, at last? And you couldn't even begin to imagine all the things you wouldn't be able to do in public for fear of jeopardizing Mad's situation, like look at a guy in the street or turn around as he walked by or give out your phone number or kiss a guy in public or take him home. No matter how often Mad said to you that you could be a free couple, nothing would ever be that easy again, and the more you thought about it, the more the territory of forbidden things seemed to expand. One night you had these terrible nightmares which made you scream so loud that you woke up. Mad was at your bedside, and there was such a terribly sad smile on that face you know by heart.

At the end of our last year of lycée, Mad's father, who worked in Mali, had an accident on a construction site, a fatal accident. It was just after our philosophy exam, (Does becoming self-aware mean one becomes a stranger to oneself?), and the Arabesque, Mad and I were pleased with ourselves because we had successfully met the challenge that we could insert a number of words that the others had chosen for us into our essays. Mad stood there on the lawn saying, It was close, dude, shit, I thought I'd never find a way to get "fennel" in there, then finally by the end, wham, I did it, straight up man, in the bag.

We slapped our palms together and went on home, where Mommydaddy told me we were a bunch of childish idiots because I told them I'd managed to insert "stag" and "ballot" and Mad had gotten away with "Disneyland" and "fennel," but the Arabesque failed because Mad had given her "fellatio" and "quartz."

Later that day, early evening, Mad came over and he was weeping. He had tears on his T-shirt that said, *Save a Tree, Eat a Beaver.*

That was the first time in your life you had ever seen Mad cry and it was a really weird feeling because you cried but Mad never did. You were the one who went weepy watching *The Land Before Time, E.T., Armageddon, Titanic* and more recently *Summer Palace, The Old Garden,* and *As Tears Go By* because you *loved* Asian movies, but that had only started about six months earlier.

I had him come in through the door at the side of the house, the one that Mommydaddy couldn't see from the living room, the one Mad always used when he wanted to get them worried, as if he were some lover sneaking out of my closet, and I sat him down on the big bed in the playroom. For two hours he wept and couldn't speak and he tore up his Kleenexes whenever he tried to wipe his eyes or his nose. When he finally calmed down he told me he was going back to Mali, that he wanted to leave right away, even though his mother had said he mustn't come back until he'd passed his baccalaureate exams, and he wouldn't even be there for his father's funeral, and his mother told him that his father wouldn't want him to fail his exams, the dead were dead and the living must think about the future.

I said, Will you stay there all summer?

—I don't know when I'll be able to come back.

—Because of the visa?

—Fucking visa.

He started crying again, I took him in my arms and rocked him and he said, Hold me tighter, tighter than that, and I held him tight against my chest, we were crushing each other, so hard it took our breath away, and he said again, Hold me even tighter, Alice, so I asked him if he wanted to disappear and he said yes, this huge boy you had always seen smiling and rolling his shoulders and winking and mumbling, "Hey, touch me, blood" as he held his fist out to you, this big kid saying, Yes, disappear, and burn and melt, or dissolve into dust, because I can't think anymore, hold me closer, tight, until it hurts, I need to know if I can still feel pain. And he told me off and said I was a wuss because I let go of him after a minute had gone by because a horrible cramp was paralyzing my arm. Mad was sitting on the bed, tears everywhere, and he looked at me and I was on the floor saying, Oh fuck, fuck, shaking my right arm and trying to twist my fingers, breathing hard, waiting for the cramp to go away.

He asked, Do you remember my father?

Of course you remembered Mad's father, in your memory he was even taller than his son, his skin blacker, his eyes and teeth extraordinarily white, and in your memory he was as strong as a dozen oxen and a dozen bulls and he could lift you up, the pair of you, up to his shoulders, you on his left arm and Mad on his right, so that you could each kiss him on the cheek to wish him good night. And Mad would say, as he went off to bed, You ain't seen nothing yet, my dad is so strong that when he bends his arm to show you his muscles, they go right up to the ceiling and my mother shouts, Watch out you don't break the lamp!

You were eight years old and your eyes opened wide with admiration so Mad went on and told you that his father built houses in Mali and in France and in France it was easy because they had machinery but in Mali you had to do everything by hand, and Mad's father was the best house builder because he could shift huge blocks of stone, like in Astérix, and sometimes when people wanted to move house he could pull a whole house off its foundations and just put it on the truck and the driver would say, Mister, you really are the strongest, I don't know how we'd manage without you, and Mad's father hardly even wiped his forehead and he would say, *It's my pleasure,* in English, because he learned English building a château for an American multimillionaire.

You remembered Mad's father coming into the bathroom when you and Mad were having a bloodthirsty battle in the tub. You were making terrible typhoons of snow with the bubbles, hurling it onto his squadron of flying toothbrushes and shouting, Drat, I'm done for! like in the film on TV the night before, and just when your blizzard was about to land right on Mad's army, he turned into a submarine and managed to submerge just in time to escape your magic spell. His father waited for him to lift his head out of the water—which Mad did in no time at all because he had foam in his eyes and he was shouting, I'm blind, I'm blind! And his dad said, The water belongs *in* the bathtub, kids, not next to it, and anyway it's time to get out. And he grabbed the towels by the sink and held yours to the left and Mad's to the right and he counted to three. And at the count of three you both burst out of the tub and wrapped yourself up in your towels with a wail, Hurry, hurry, hurry, and you wriggled to dry your back properly and Mad's father called you Betty Boop while Mad was already trying to pull his T-shirt over his head, again saying, Hurry hurry, hurry.

Mad always won the race to be the first out of the tub and all you could do was say scornfully that he'd get mushrooms growing between his toes because he never dried his feet properly and you would rather lose than die a slow death from rotting feet. Mad's father burst out laughing and ruffled your hair and told you you were a good loser, and you'd be having supper in the tiny little kitchen where one time Mad's big sister braided your hair the African way and you were trying not to cry because you hated having your hair pulled and most of the time when Mommydaddy tried to untangle it you would pretend to faint from the pain.

Now when I heard the news about Mad's father, all these memories came rushing back, along with the legend that Mad had created around his father—how strong he was, and heroic, and I couldn't help but imagine his accident like some huge event in an action film where Mad's father, in the middle of a flood, was trying to tear a house from the ground to keep it out of reach of the water and in the house there were little children crying and they'd lost their mother but Mad's father winked at them and told them that everything was going to be all right and he could even hold the house up on his back with one arm and with his other arm he reached into his pocket to give to them some candy . . .

But then, and I could almost see it, after he put the house

back down in a safe place, on a dry riverbank, he noticed another house with a little old lady holding her cat in her arms and he went back again and again until the fatigue nearly over-whelmed him, and just then there came a terrible typhoon with snow and bits of houses and maybe even cows all whirling around and Mad's father was struck in the head by a roof and he fell stunned into the black boiling water and no one, of all the villagers he had saved, was strong enough to manage to get him out of there.

I never asked Mad exactly what had happened, and Mad never told me either. Only once did I hear Mad's mother talk about *that death machine* but deep down I don't want to know.

Roughly one month before the ceremony, Mad moved into my place, my little apartment in the tenth arrondissement, and you decided to stay roommates until the end of the marriage and the lie, and to find a bigger apartment as soon as you could, because he was sleeping on your sofa, but *matrimonial cohabitation* was an obvious requirement.

If it weren't for this constant impression of faking it, it would be a pleasure to live with your lifelong friend who cooks like no one on earth. Sometimes you put the music on really loud to dance all over the place, on the table and chairs and his erstwhile sofa bed. The Arabesque and Jérémie come over a lot too because they're the only ones you don't have to hide the marriage from, or lie to, or talk about love, they won't wonder why you don't kiss, and you don't have to put away the blankets that are flung around the living room to make them believe you're sleeping together.

Like in the lycée years we watch movies and dream up imaginary scenarios, and like in the lycée years we smoke joints, even though I stopped years ago, and we lend each other books and sometimes when neither of us has the strength to move we order these huge pizzas and eat them while we watch some inane trash on the box and laugh. It would be really really great to be sharing this with Mad if it weren't for the concierge every morning calling us the lovebirds and we don't know what to say. Then there was that incident one night.

I went out with the Arabesque and Petite, a friend from

university, and she took us to the Troisième Lieu on the Rue Quincampoix. It was a place we went to a lot because the Arabesque and I loved to play table soccer and shriek a lot really loud and break the rules, so much so that Mad had refused to play with us for years. There was no other place besides the Troisième Lieu where girls could have fun on their own, and the music was great, and anyway I liked the place. Except that it was a lesbian bar. Which had never been a problem before.

That night, it was another great evening, and the Arabesque and I were absolutely pounding these two enormous kind of scary girls who had clearly delineated muscles on their naked arms, and whenever we scored a goal we were afraid they might come storming over at us with a raging fist, but in the end they said we weren't much to look at. And they bought us beers which we all drank perfectly cheerfully, although we noticed we'd lost Petite because she'd run off with a pretty Japanese girl.

I got back to the apartment feeling proud and a little tipsy and I told Mad how the Arabesque's frenetic spinning had saved our bacon and I was laughing a lot. But Mad didn't seem to find it funny, listening to me. In the beginning I thought it was because he'd spent the evening here all alone with his book, and he was mad at me for having left him but then he suddenly started to tell me to cut the crap, he'd heard enough. And I went, What?

—Can't you see this is just what we've been trying to avoid from the beginning, Alice? You think that future spouses would do that sort of thing? The girl goes and hangs out in lesbian bars with friends who are obviously gay, and anyone can see as much, and she leaves her guy at home all alone and he doesn't think there's anything wrong with that? Shit, a lesbian together with an illegal—that looks even more like a *mariage blanc* than anything else we might have been afraid of.

—Do you really believe what you are saying?

—That it was a shit way to behave, yes I do believe that. What were you thinking? That I was going to cheer when I heard your score? You took a huge risk tonight, and everyone could see you!

I told him of course everyone could see me, that is, see that I was having a good time in a bar with some girlfriends, that was all, and that I'd done nothing reprehensible, but he was still pissed off and said again that I'd fucked up, fucked up big time, you hear? So after that things began to slide off the rails because I asked him who did he think he was, my father? And he said no, my future husband, and that was already plenty.

—Hey, if I'd wanted a real husband, Mad, I might have found one I was really in love with and not some jerk who's doing my head in while I'm trying to help him. If I had wanted a real husband, I would have chosen one I felt like kissing and fucking. You're not a real husband, don't you get it?

—Shout louder while you're at it, fuck, I don't think the neighbors could hear you!

I lowered my voice but I went on telling him that he had no right, absolutely no right at all to reproach me in that way, and I was angry and drunk, and drunk with anger, so I told him I wouldn't marry him if I was going to have to put up with scenes like that, and this marriage was simply taking my whole life away from me, and I wouldn't have anything left, no friends, no love affairs, if he turned into some paranoid asshole, and what would he do if one day during those four years I met someone, would he stop me seeing him or walking down the street with him? Or lock me up in a cellar for as long as it took him to get his nationality? And I asked him, Who are you, Bluebeard? Was he hiding the corpses of all the women he'd married before me and who had failed to obey the rules of the great lie of a *mariage blanc*?

While I was talking I was throwing the books that were

lying around onto the floor, and I think I was about to start on the glasses but Mad had already broken so many since he moved in that I remembered at the last minute that they were too rare to be given that sort of treatment. I paced the room, furiously pointing my finger at him, and he was sitting on the sofa with his head in his hands saying over and over, God what a load of shit, not only you behave like shit but you're full of it as well.

We shouted at each other for maybe half an hour, taking a break now and then to roll a cigarette, but then one of us always looked up and said, And you know what else? and off we went again.

I said, Ayatollah, selfish, bastard, after everything I've done for you, I would never have believed it, you dirty rotten selfish bastard. He said, Then don't do it, go on, think about your comfortable little life, if this is too much to ask of you, you're afraid to help out, you're just some bourgeois chick, know what, don't do it, you're just a dirty Marie-Amélie in disguise, I would never have believed it, after everything we've been through together.

In the end I was crying but I went on speaking and insulting him, and his eyes were bloodshot from cigarette smoke. We were pathetic.

Up to that point you still went on hoping it wouldn't change anything and that Mad and you would still be the same blood siblings you'd been since nursery school, that this would turn out to be just some big joke, but that night you realized it wasn't possible.

I went off to bed without forgiving him, without asking him to forgive me either, I just didn't get it. And as I left him there on the creaking sofa—because naturally you'd broken the springs from jumping up and down whenever one of you started watching *The Arcade Fire*—I almost wished that we were a real couple after all, with skin that had been touched and caressed, because then all it would take would be for me to turn back and look at him, from the door, and say with all our reconciliations in my voice, You coming to bed? And Mad would follow me and we'd make awesome reconciliation love of the kind so highly vaunted by *Sex and the City* or the readers of *Glamour* magazine.

But a *mariage blanc* doesn't allow for the corporal healing of conflict, and I wasn't of an age to reach out a fraternal hand and say, Peace? So all I could do was slam the bedroom door hard as I could behind me, but not soon enough to avoid seeing Mad's middle finger raised in my direction.

Never again would we mention the Troisième Lieu.

If someone asked you today how far back your ideas about the Great History of Racism went, you would say you must have started getting them in around 2007. Because before then you hadn't really started gathering the evidence. And besides, you must realize, before it concerned Mad directly you didn't really have any reason to complain about the fate the Great History had allotted to you. Of course you always proudly and loudly proclaimed your *Algéritude,* to a far greater degree than your little Africa birthmark might have warranted, but you would have to agree that most of the time you were an itinerant rip-off artist on the topic. In 2007 you became a true historian, and you unearthed all the files. And the Arabesque gratified you with the flattering nickname of Alice, alias the Memory.

That was the year that Mad started having major problems with the Préfecture, and the political climate did not bode well, either. It was a presidential election year, and there in the middle of all the campaign ads for candidates whom Mad, the Arabesque and I, from our posts hovering over the papers and three cups of coffee, took immense pleasure in painstakingly demolishing, there in the middle of all the promises that no one listened to, and all the completely demagogical campaign platforms, there was suddenly talk of creating a new Ministry.

The first time it came on the scene Nicolas Sarkozy introduced it himself, and no one had, as yet, added the words "integration" or "fostering solidarity" which were supposed to round off the edges,[1] no, in the beginning it was just the "Ministry of Immigration and National Identity," and the two terms seemed poised, from either corner of the new term, to launch into a ruthless boxing match, to rip apart those capital I's and tear out all the n's, and when Mad burst into the café next to the Censier métro where I always had a drink after class and put the paper with its headline down before me, he said, I'm fucked, man, I'm fucked.

And he was right that day, over the beer I bought him, when he asserted that this sort of announcement would hardly stop anyone from voting for Sarkozy. I absorbed the information with the benevolent smile of someone who knows that the Right doesn't stand a chance. I turned the paper over to hide the article and I handed the saucer of peanuts to Mad and reassured him.

That was your major problem all through 2007—your optimism, your confidence—and it was all the fault of your date of birth: you'd been born and raised a socialist, you were a little princess of the Mitterrand reign. There was a part of you that refused to believe that France could be anything but a left-wing country. You had thought Chirac was just a one-off, a mistake compounded by a forced ballot, but now France had had twelve years to realize it was a left-wing country: how could it fail to see what was obvious?

But as the months went by, my smile began to feel forced as I followed the polls and watched the debates and heard the people around me saying give him a chance before you condemn him and maybe, just maybe, I would be surprised to see how he could change the country.

Yes, I ended up discovering just how wrong I had been, just

[1] "Ministère de l'Immigration, de l'Intégration, de l'Identité nationale et du Développement solidaire": created in May, 2007, it was dissolved in November, 2010, after considerable public criticism. (T.N.)

how much I had confused enthusiasm with political analysis, because that blade was about to fall as well.

France was a right-wing country: 53% of the ballot said as much.

It was the month of May, 2007, and my democratic sentiment would not allow me to go and join the others at the Bastille to demand the dissolution of the Ministry, and my innate respect of property would not allow me to go and burn other people's cars. And yet I almost felt like it. Instead of staying home and watching television, all those people marching to pat themselves on the back and that woman touching herself to point out all the parts of her body where she can feel the thrill of the election results, all those who hope for something from the ministries with a knowing air.

It was on that rotten screen, its picture blurred in all four corners, that I saw Brice Hortefeux for the first time. I was immediately struck by how white his skin was, and I could not understand how anyone could fail to realize the terrible significance of their gesture and go on to entrust the Ministry of Immigration and National Identity to such a paragon of whiteness.

I wanted to tear myself from my contemplation of the TV screen, but I couldn't. I sat there on the floor in the middle of the living room and I looked at *them*, on the Place de la Concorde, as they dove in the fountains and brushed aside the blond bangs hanging in their face, with an irritated gesture, as they marched along in their pin-striped shirts, dazzling their eyes with the brilliance of their watches and their shining teeth, ecstatically brandishing their champagne glasses, conceiving the first gleaming babies of *Sarkozysme* on the hoods of their cars, tearing the spaghetti straps of their silk dresses, applauding, shouting, emerging in a horde from under the Pont Alexandre-III, heading into the harsh light of the fireworks and diving again and again as if every fountain in Paris had been transformed into a pool of champagne by virtue of the single miracle of an election.

I knew only one thing, felt only one thing: those people were raising their glasses to Mad's departure. I took every one of their smiles as a personal affront, every shout as a personal aggression. I locked myself in, turning the key twice, feeling clandestine, to stay in denial just a bit longer, rolling myself up in the comforter, not answering the phone, just watching the same images over and over, and at the bottom of the screen was the ticker listing the results by town and I swore that I would not set foot again in over half of France.

The next morning Mad almost broke my door down to bring me croissants and he told me that a woman in the métro had said to him, Ah, not so proud now, are we, when all he was doing was looking for his ticket in his jacket pocket. I burst into tears.

In the end, all that the Great Inquisition was good for was to make you dangerously worried, and it drove you to reveal various secrets that you would otherwise have kept to yourselves for twenty years.

Because in reality there was no Edvige, no light shining mercilessly into your eyes, no guy smoking and typing on a typewriter in a dark corner while his colleague stood loosening his tie, the better to hit you.

Sitting across from me was a big blonde woman, and she smiled and said, I really hate having to do this. She was wearing a sky blue tweed suit, completely inappropriate for the season, and her little office was permeated by a strong scent of blackberry, her terribly sweet perfume, while Mad waited out in the corridor and I was the first to go.

Have a seat, she said, pointing to a plastic chair, and I sat down awkwardly, absolutely certain the moment I made contact with the seat that I would leave circles of sweat when I stood up again. Just then I was so afraid, while she was playing with her pen and leafing through her papers.

—So you want to get married?

It was such a simple question that I couldn't help but think it must be a trap and that she was hiding a lie detector under the desk, or that she was checking to see whether my pupils were dilating. And then I pulled myself together, and reassured myself that in any event my reply could only ever be the truth, *I do yes I do.*

I want to marry Mad.

—At your age?

I would have liked to know whether she had asked Jean Sarkozy the same question, because he was even younger than me when all the newspaper posters on the ceiling of the métro announced his engagement.

—I feel like I've known him all my life.

I borrowed most of my answers from the testimonies of *Cosmopolitan* readers. Mad had dug his fingers into his throat pretending to vomit when he saw me studiously reading those magazines. But with the blonde woman it seemed to work. She shook her bracelets with a flick of her wrist and gave me a simpering smile, I see, of course.

—What sort of work does he do?

I told her about the shoes, all the boxes of multicolored tennis shoes on the Boulevard Raspail, and how he wanted to go back to school. I said, You know, he was really smart at the lycée, but the world is so unfair, and with the economic crisis on top of it, everyone takes what they can get, if only he could have made it through his final year I am sure, I am positive he could have done better than me at university, easily.

Another shake of the bracelets. With a laugh. You're being modest. The École Normale Supérieure, after all . . . I silently thanked Mommydaddy for having urged me to take the entrance exams, which the blonde lady seemed to consider a pledge of good conduct. She viewed the book sticking out of my bag differently now. My nephew took the exams, too, she said. Clinking sound as she lowered her arm to the desk. She was silent for a few seconds then said, The economic crisis, of course. Do you live together?

In fifteen minutes she wrapped up the session, all harmless questions and not one about our sexual habits. It was almost frustrating to have practiced so hard, and then that was it. A victory without peril is a joyless triumph, indeed. You had imagined for so long how the two of you would come out of that office and run down the middle of the street, eyes ablaze with victory, shouting, jumping, slicing open your champagne bottle with an enormous scimitar.

But the enemy was being too conciliatory, far too tender. She didn't even know she was the enemy as she innocently handed me a packet of half-melted nougats, confessing that she loved the things, and then she went on to the next question, laughing because her mouth was still full, Oh they do stick to your teeth these things, don't they, forgive me.

When the interview was over she stood up and again said that she hated, absolutely hated having to do this, and she added, Gracious, after all, when anyone sees the two of you, so young, so good-looking, they would really have to have something wrong with them to ever doubt you really want to be together.

Which goes to show that even a registrar of vital statistics was prepared to go along with Mad's physical compatibility ranking system.

So I gave a phony little laugh and said Of course, of course, goodbye, and I waved to my potential husband that it was his turn to go into the office.

Now I was the one out in the hall but I wasn't afraid the way Mad had been afraid because I knew he'd give all the right answers, about my eating habits, and my pets, and the description of our bedroom, Do you have plans, do you want children, why are you getting married so young? The blonde lady, that was all she wanted, to hear his answers, and she'd nod her head, and nod her bracelets, for her whole being was nothing but approval of our couple and our love, and with a complicit little laugh she would also offer Mad some treats and she would have that splendid nostalgic smile on her face when, like me, he would say that we wanted to have some more fun together just the two of us before having Héloïse and Alexandre three or four years from now.

Everything was going so unexpectedly smoothly, which could only be to the good, and yet . . . In the eggshell-colored corridor there was something not quite right. I did not feel good. It had been so easy to lie to the fat blonde lady, watching as she patted her hair. That was all she dreamt of, love stories like ours. She must watch them on television every night, and maybe even during her lunch break, reveling in them on the sly on her computer.

You felt sad for her sake. Not for lying to her, no, but for not being able to give her an authentic passionate love story with all the necessary trimmings, from the flowers to the violin.

You felt sad for all the people who really do love each other and to whom this sort of investigation is an insult, couples who genuinely deserve an investigator as understanding as the plump lady. Because in the end maybe all you and Mad deserved was Edvige, an inhumane entity you could deceive with pleasure, who wouldn't wish you all the joy in the world and who wouldn't say, They will be lovely, in response to your answer to her question about children. An Edvige who wouldn't think Mad was handsome, just black. Who would justify all your hatred of the ministry and its laws on immigration. Not a plump blonde lady who ate nougat in secret in her office, and chocolate *macarons* as she sat weeping in front of her soaps.

You mused that maybe the blonde lady had a black lover when she was young and that her parents stopped her from seeing him and maybe she took this job to save all the couples she possibly could in the name not of political action, no way, but of Love Without Borders and Colors. You thought that maybe the blonde lady had tears in her eyes whenever she saw a black man and a white woman together, or a little mixed-race kid, and she would dream of what her fate might have been if one night her father hadn't started shouting at the dinner table and hadn't said to her erstwhile lover, If you ever so much as try and see my daughter again, you'll be in deep trouble, believe me.

And maybe she wanted to go against her parents and find him, and maybe she told him she would run away with him, that she would follow him anywhere, and maybe she said, Meet me at midnight in the garden behind the house, and she climbed out the little skylight with her suitcase and her traveling coat but when she got to the garden she saw him and he didn't have a suitcase. He whispered very quietly for a long time, explaining to her that he would never forgive himself if she were to break off with her family so brutally, because after all, blood ties are forever, and you and me, who knows, maybe in six months we won't even be in love anymore, you won't love me because I was the one who tore you away from your family and your country, or it may just turn out that love fades. The blonde lady swore it wasn't true, she'd never, ever, have such petty thoughts, no, not her, they would love one another, but he said it again, Believe me, believe me, we mustn't, I can't. So they were both weeping, and he was saying farewell, farewell, and, Thank you, thank you always, when I saw you climbing down from the roof with your suitcase it was the most beautiful thing I have ever seen, and it will always be the most beautiful thing, go back to your family who love you, they don't know me, they can't understand, but they do love you, go back to your warm room and your little girl's bed, I will never forget you. The blonde lady was in tears and she let him go, felt his hand slipping away from hers, watched him leave and disappear around the corner, while her suitcase hung uselessly from her hand against her leg. She went around the house to go in the front door, and she walked silently through the living room and up the stairs and when she sat down on her bed, weeping, her mother opened the door and saw the suitcase. She said, Are you going away? But the blonde lady said, No, no, on the contrary. Her mother sat down next to her, she didn't understand, and the blonde lady was sobbing as she said, Oh, mom, it is so hard, and her mother gently stroked her hair and held her in her arms and said, Give it time, it takes time, you'll see, it will pass, everything will be fine, you will be happy.

But the blonde lady had never forgotten.

I must really have been feeling weird in that corridor to have dreamt all that up in the twenty minutes Mad was in there, and when he came out, I was so upset by the story that I threw myself in his arms so desperately you would think we really were those lovers the fat lady thought she had helped. And her smile when she saw the two of us in each other's arms made me think that I must have been completely right about that whole business.

But it was not something I ever found out.

On May 15, at the end of the afternoon, there was a stormy wind blowing, of the kind that gives you a headache. It was a shitty day, one of those days when you're sad for no reason, whether it's because the world is in a bad way or your shoelace has come undone. Everything seemed to weigh so heavily, from your legs to your nostalgia for some vague yesteryear, something you may not even have experienced.

For as long as you could remember (and the diary you'd been keeping since you were seven was a great help in this respect), you had always had moments like this, chronically sad moments. They would come upon you all of a sudden, even when things were fine, and they would chew you up, conscientiously. You didn't feel like doing a thing, you felt as if you'd lived for eons and already at the age of seven or twelve or fifteen you could see that you were writing about your long experience of life and your imminent death with the same gravitas.

By then I was an adult and yet the fact that I'd been through several such phases, where life seemed to have shown me all there was and could only go on in a state of decline and loss, did not leave me any less attentive to the little music of all the violins in the world. You idiot, you knew damn well: it must have been the hundredth time you'd let sadness catch you unawares as you walked out of the kitchen, and instead of just shrugging your shoulders you welcomed it with open arms.

I was in my living room, with the orange sofa sagging underneath me, and I was thinking about everything I'd lived through over these last years and would never know ever again. All the towns I'd lived in where now I would never be anything more than a tourist, all the people I'd been close to because we lived near one another—the neighbors on the landing, schoolmates, compatriots who had gone abroad and who now were relegated to electronic address books, the café proprietors who used to greet me by name and serve me my *bière blanche* with a wedge of lemon, the bus that crossed all of Paris to take me home from the Rue de la Duée, and the campfires in the green belt which nearly always resulted in a visit from the police.

An entire collection of tiny, insignificant memories, the kind that you don't take pictures of, like the way your old apartment used to smell, and how you'd close the shutters at night, the little garden outside the building that smelled of rain and damp earth, the dark leaves shining under the streetlamps.

The cherry tree outside your balcony, two years later; Mad biting off the cherries, leaning over the railing, not even removing them first from the tree.

Blocks of ice drifting down the river as far as the eye could see.

The naked arms of the boy from across the way when he would stand in the courtyard and do his juggling.

Of course I could go back there, see the buildings again, see my studio that has been converted into a garage for two-wheeled vehicles, maybe even go up to the second floor and say hi to the old neighbors. But when you go back somewhere that used to belong to you, for no other reason than memory, that's what makes you feel like a stranger to the place, that's what leaves you with a feeling that you've lost your home, not your Africa birthmark or the yellow poster in the métro saying, *Now you can call Algeria*, as if Algeria might pick up and answer and say, Hello, Alice? Is that you? Is that really you at last?

It's never the same, when you go back. As if you could only experience something the first time round. And after the first second has gone by, it's already the past.

Like all the boys and men you can count on more than the fingers of both hands and with whom you can never experience those times again. You can't relive an affair. You can only see someone again.

I sat lost in thought on my orange sofa. All the ones I'd like to meet again for the first time, and the ones with whom I'd like to relive that first instant, the discovery of their smile, or the way they'd say my name or tell me about their life so convincingly that I would buy it all, even when the months that followed only served to deconstruct the palace of their legend; and the ones from whom I waited for a first kiss, that moment when our lips would be a hundredth of an inch apart and your entire brain was nothing but a violent command, *go on* screaming inside you, and the moment they bit their lips during orgasm, and the moment they said *I love you* for the first time, on a haystack next to my lycée, or outside Notre-Dame cathedral.

Of course you could go back and see them, see that their arms no longer hold your shape, lie down on their pillows that have lost your perfume, read half the books on their shelves that you gave them, with your written dedication. You could even say it again, I love you, but there would no longer be that expectancy, that search for a clue, and besides, now you know how they fuck, and the way they say your name would only turn your guts inside out because of all the memories, even the one whose voice was so deep that his messages on the answering machine used to distort the bass. Memory dulls the blade of pain, braces your heart, gives a soft bed to the space of love.

To return to a foreign place when all you want is a home; to return to conquered territory when, really, you want to start over and ride into battle: that's a non-return, a fake return. Either way it's no go. All those places you've left behind, you've lost them for good.

The list was too long that day. I looked at photographs and reread passages in my diary. Flashes of names and faces. I remembered the love they conjured, and the dresses I had dared to wear, and I hated myself, especially that green one with the sequined flower on the shoulder.

In short, it was one of those days when a crying jag was inevitable, almost systematic, because every word had already been said in other circumstances, every word echoed with past use and made the years expand painfully.

When Mad showed up, carrying a big shopping bag over his shoulder, he found me curled up under my blanket with the photographs scattered all over the table and a half-empty box of tissues. He carried the milk cartons and fruit juice into the kitchen and crouching down in front of the fridge he asked me what was going on.

—I've been thinking about Before.

Mad knew me so well that he could hear the capital letter and he didn't ask before what but let out an appreciative whistle between his teeth and said, That sucks, man.

—I was thinking, the longer you live, the more people you lose. How many of our friends from the lycée do we still see?

—Not a whole lot, hummed Mad.

I could hear him in the kitchen getting annoyed with the vegetable crisper and then he came over and lay down next to me on the sofa.

—We've still got the best ones.

—Jérem and the Arabesque?

—Yup. And you and me, above all.

I laughed quietly.

—Yes, you and me, we're the best. For sure.

Mad gave some thought to Before then said it was this sort of thing that had made the owners of Facebook so rich.

Could be, but behind the stupidity of all the tests and the selling of friends, behind the "what sort of underwear are you?", maybe there was a deeper logic. Maybe we were all there because we were scared sick of losing each other, and that way we were able to keep a little bit of control over the lives we'd encountered. It wasn't a means of communication, in fact, but a way of collecting the people you did not want to believe had left your life for good. People you patiently kept your eye on, and spied on thanks to their photos and their status, and from time to time you might leave a comment on their wall, just to get the impression that, well sure, they were still a part of your life. When you clicked on "Like," or when you followed links from album to album, from friend to friend to friend, through tags and "crêpe parties," it was simply so you wouldn't have to say goodbye. Maybe behind all the profiles and all the questions of "What are you doing now?" there was a terrible fear. One we all shared.

—They ought to put dead people on Facebook, too, said Mad, because they belong there, too.

And then he fell silent. His father. His father's face. Lost for good. I cursed myself.

But Mad wasn't sad, Mad was smiling softly and he said, Ah . . . to start crying because of Before . . . That's just typical prenuptial hen party behavior.

—Yeah, right, I sighed, picking up the photographs on the table.

—I'm not joking, mam'selle. You haven't forgotten you're going to be my white bride tomorrow?

I shrugged. How could I forget. And then I asked him if he was really going to celebrate that evening.

—The Arabesque and Jérémie will be here in a quarter of an hour.

I looked at all my dirty tissues, my pajama bottoms, and my worn flip-flops that used to have daisies on the soles.

—I don't want them to see me like this.

Mad pretended not to hear and said again that I had a quarter of an hour. Then twelve minutes. Then ten. I finally headed for the bathroom.

It was nine o'clock at night. In less than twenty-four hours I would be married to Mad. And I would have liked to slip my fingers behind the Plexiglas clock face to prevent the hands from turning. Because they were moving too quickly.

It was nine o'clock on May 15, 2009. The Arabesque and Jérémie had already lit the oven to reheat the pork buns from the usual Chinese canteen. Mad prepared a bowl of ice cubes and brought out all the half-empty bottles. I was the only one doing nothing, sitting on the sofa, practically paralyzed.

I listened with one ear to Jérémie's umpteenth tirade against the RATP; he wants public transport to be free. Zero euro, zero fraud. I couldn't join in.

Because neither Jérémie nor the Arabesque were about to get married to Mad the next day. Only me. And the usual slogans about all our way-cool left-wing youth militancy seemed utterly senseless to me. As did the amount of the fine in the métro, compared with the sharp edges of sugar cubes in women's prisons and the pathological fear I have of getting my eye poked out. Oozing with pus.

I almost felt like killing them for sitting there so calmly— wasn't Mad afraid, shouldn't he be afraid like me, instead of stuffing himself on munchies?

Couldn't we just talk about this fucking *mariage blanc* instead of pretending to be a bunch of friends having a drink before dinner?

Finally the Arabesque broached the subject, pulling a pair

of new shoes from her huge shoulder bag and saying that she was ready, she had her outfit for tomorrow.

—Heels, get a load of that, said Mad.

There was surprise in his voice and I couldn't help but look at the shoes and join, if not in the conversation, in the general mood, which was one of universal surprise in fact, because no one has ever, ever, seen the Arabesque perched on high heels. In her book heels are borderline unethical.

As the three of us gaped at her, the Arabesque began to stammer that she figured that, well, she thought, because in a way . . . She stopped, took her time, took a deep breath, and suddenly blurted, We have to be a part of it, every one of us, we have to contribute . . . How can I put it? Do our bit for the Great Lie. Because tomorrow is our opportunity, now or never. So I wondered how I could be there with my entire being, not just as a witness signing the book . . . be there to make you understand that you have my support, for your weird sort of holy matrimony, and I can imagine this is not easy for you, and your sense of integrity must be taking a beating somewhere along the line . . .

Mad didn't take his eyes off her, and he still had a surprised look on his face when he said, Well, yeah, but why heels? And Jérémie and I both nodded to say that we just didn't see what that was supposed to prove.

—Because it's a lie! exclaimed the Arabesque, blushing a little, it's against my very nature to pretend to be the kind of girl who wears heels. And I figured it was sort of the equivalent of the marriage itself, because in the end it's the Great Lie that is turning everything we've been for years into some sort of romantic or glamorous schmaltz, so if we can say, get a load of this, Mad and Alice are madly in love, we can also say that the Arabesque loves to teeter around on her stilettos . . .

She seemed unsure herself, about how valid her reasoning was, but since we were laughing, she sighed, Well, what do I know . . .

And the four of us together finished by saying, Yeah, what does anyone know.

But the Arabesque's gesture, however pointless, did make me feel good. First of all because I really needed to know that evening that someone—as the clock hands turned, inexorably—realized that it wasn't necessarily easy for me to marry Mad, and it wasn't like going to stick up posters or calling for a demonstration. And because for the Arabesque civil disobedience took the shape of a pair of duck blue stilettos, and that really made me laugh. And finally because at last we were talking about the wedding and the fact that it was the very next day.

I agreed to taste some of the leftover booze, so Mad made me a cocktail, his own concoction, called "Autumn Rose" because of the suspicious brownish color and sweet, cloying taste: "But the mud is made of our flowers," he said, quoting Queneau with a learned air.

The night wore on, D-Day had arrived a few minutes earlier when the Arabesque ventured to ask whether we thought our romantic futures would be completely compromised for the next four years.

How often I had wished I could talk it over with her, when the fear woke me up in the night, when I'd met some guy who was particularly fine or when my neighbor on the bench at university asked for my phone number. But for months it had been a taboo subject and the Arabesque had never brought it up, she avoided it, was clever at dodging it, even clammed up completely if she suspected that's what I was referring to.

That evening she explained at last, making big circles with her arms which regularly threatened the cushions with a downpour of Autumn Rose. She said, I was worried I'd scare you, sweetie, that I might cause you to desert, and it would have been targeting Mad if I'd done that, and I figured that if you had never thought about it then I might be planting doubts in your mind.

—But of course I think about it, fuck, I've been thinking about it all the time . . .

I didn't go any further, for fear my voice might break, for fear of hurting Mad too, because he was already feeling vulnerable, and his hand commiserated on the back of my neck and his thumb was playing with my hair and asking for forgiveness. I tried to flash him my best "no sweat, dude" smile, but I'm not sure it worked.

—And what about the future? asked Jérémie, and we couldn't really hold it against him because it's true that when Mad was around Jérémie's sex appeal rank always went up and he must have been afraid that this charmed period would come to an end.

And it would. And tough luck, too, Jérémie. He should have just married Mad himself if he didn't like it.

Mad laughed and said well, okay, the future wasn't looking exactly radiant but it wasn't completely compromised either because all we had to do was be very careful who we hung out with, and only go out with decent people in the presence of decent people.

—You'll get to scream, "Quick, hide in the closet, I hear my husband coming!" said the Arabesque, her eyes full of admiration.

And I grunted something to the effect that the number of decent people and risk-free situations was probably pretty limited.

Then Jérémie said, So basically what it means is, zero risk, Mad, you go out with my sister, and Alice . . .

Huge smile, right up to his swimming-pool-blue eyes:

—You'll have to make do with me.

I only just managed to keep up with the general laughter and sigh, Great, thanks, when they all fell silent. It was ten past midnight and I felt like killing everyone all over again.

After all, it was not just one way of life that was coming to an end, but two, and it wasn't the sort of thing you can do and not feel sad and abandoned as you leave corpses behind you. So maybe it was normal I felt like murdering someone, normal that my mood was swinging from despair to hysterical joy and that the evening had been so strange overall, until we all fell into each other's arms swearing eternal love and friendship, and we thought we were really grand, and what we were doing surpassed even the French Revolution or May '68, and we decreed it was the finest manifestation of pacifist terrorism.

It was two minutes past two when we went with the Arabesque and Jérémie to the door and said, Be sure you show up tomorrow, it's twelve hours from now, and Jérémie and Mad were each singing their own drunken version of *La Marseillaise* on either side of the door, something about tall ferocious blacks coming into our midst to marry our daughters and our consorts.

I went automatically to check my dress on its hanger and my two black shoes neatly lined up before heading for my not at all marital bed, and I suddenly thought that maybe this was Jérémie's last chance to prevent the marriage, by confessing his love to me, and that maybe right that instant he was bounding up the stairs four at a time, there was still time, and I was about to hear the sound of footsteps and a mad pressing of the buzzer because he was in such a hurry and so eager and I would hardly have time to open the door, but the minutes ticked by—fucking wall clock—in almost total silence, and Mad finally got up to switch off the light and said, Go to bed, *now.*

And I obeyed, in a torpor that was due largely to the amount of Autumn Rose flowing through my veins. Before I dropped off I still had time to screen the Great History of Racism one last time, from the sandbox to the hordes of the army of Evil waiting for Mad at the Préfecture, and time to think that I was doing the right thing, and then immediately afterwards that I was making a monumental mistake.

But I knew I would say it, all the same. I would say *I do yes I do.*

It is two thirty-five P.M. on May 16, 2009. I come out of the *mairie*, still clinging to Mad's arm as if the simple warmth of his skin through the cloth will give meaning to the ever-so-brief ceremony that has just taken place in the *mairie* of the tenth arrondissement—without a shout, without an interruption or a legion of envoys from the Ministry of Immigration to stop us. In the middle of the street the little girls with their pink pigtails and the woman in the multicolored madras dress are still there—and when I think I got married that quick, that the people waiting for the 38 bus when I went in were still there when I came out, it gives me a strange feeling, of distortion.

That's all it took for Mad and me to seal our alliance of friendship. We didn't manage to do it by buying the Château of Versailles—it's too bad but you have to admit it was too expensive—but by joining our two names to create a two-headed *Super-Bougnoule* entity, ZeniterTraoré, almost as indivisible as Mommydaddy. Perhaps those few minutes were all it took, too, to root Mad to French soil, and maybe his next application will go smoothly, since I've done all I can to protect him with the umbrella of my nationality and the blue color of my ID card— and since we have the same golden ring around our fingers.

—In two days the color will start coming off, warned Jérémy; he's the one who bought them.

And now that it's done, I feel almost lighthearted as I come down the steps, and I even manage to smile to my sisters, who are heading off to the station to go back to Mommydaddy out in the country, and to the Arabesque who has taken her camera out again, and to Jérémie who is tossing handfuls of rice at us from a packet he has hastily torn open.

I know that the *Super-Bougnoule* will have its share of problems, too—Mad and I have thought through all the issues raised by our new, doubly African name, and it may give us a hard time getting an apartment, or simply mean that there will be twice as much surface now for the blows that will surely come from the Great History of Racism. But I won't worry about the future. Not now. No, please. In my mind the *Super-Bougnoule* is sure to have super-powers that will protect us from everything, like strangler-threads woven in its carpets or mini-revolvers in its bananas.

It's done. I said *I do yes I do I do* and Mad said *I do yes indeed I do*, in sickness and in health, and the Arabesque swore *yes indeed they do*, until death do us part, and there was the portrait of the president on the wall and he seemed to know we were lying, but it's his fault too if the Great History got us carted us off to the *mairie* of the tenth arrondissement for a shotgun wedding between two runs of the 38 bus.

I do yes I do and there was this strange moment when they said, "You may now kiss the bride," and Mad and I started laughing irrepressibly and couldn't stop. Because it couldn't help but remind us of being teenagers and those stupid party games—the famous spin-the-bottle—which inevitably ended up like that. And I knew perfectly well as I held my lips out to him that Mad too must be thinking back to when we were fifteen, and our early days at the lycée, and the timed kiss we had to give each other, and how after the official minute was over the girl behind me had asked wasn't it weird since we both had such big lips, and we laughed, and I said, To be honest, it's kind of soft, and Mad said, It's plush, like a pillow. So now when Mad leaned toward me I almost expected to see the Arabesque or the mayor click on their stopwatches and I started laughing even harder, even with his lips on mine, savoring mine, and our teeth were touching because when Mad laughs he always laughs with a wide grin. And it was done.

My legs start to feel like jelly as we walk away. Our couple is falling to bits already, my arm slips from Mad's, I slow down to let the Arabesque catch up with me and Jérémie has started walking faster alongside Mad, slapping him soundly in the back. As we start heading up the Rue du Château-d'Eau, leaving behind all the hair stylists shaving spirals on guys' heads and weaving rainbows in women's, leaving behind the Chinese nail salons where they give you fake nails decorated with tropical islands, with a single gaze I can see them all looking at me: my childhood friend, my husband for a day, my best buddy, my witness, my love of the lycée years, all my accomplices in the very long lie, and with the same gaze I see the streets of Paris that belong to us, that belong to all our wanderings and that will lead to all the adventurous possibilities awaiting the *Super-Bougnoule*. And I'm overwhelmed by a kind of innocent joy, of the Famous Five variety, at the mere thought of it.

From now on—I also savor this thought, and savor it all the more given the fact that in the Rue du Château-d'Eau all my neighbors called me Snow White, completely overlooking my birthmark—my invisible, innate *Algéritude* will be reinforced by Mad's presence, by the risk I've taken to bind myself to his *Africanité*: from now on I really will have one foot in Africa.

So I open my mouth to the sky of the tenth arrondissement and let out the kind of triumphant ululation that only a *Super-Bougnoule* can make on great ceremonial occasions. And Mad barks, and Jérémie shouts, and the Arabesque paws the ground, and in the left-hand corner of a cloud high in the sky I wonder if that isn't Mommydaddy I can see up there, flying past at full speed, looking for some new injustice to fight.

Europa Editions publishes in the US and in the UK. Not all titles are available in both countries. Availability of individual titles is indicated in the following list.

Carmine Abate
Between Two Seas
"A moving portrayal of generational continuity."
—*Kirkus Reviews*
224 pp • $14.95 • 978-1-933372-40-2 • Territories: World

The Homecoming Party
"A sincere novel that examines the bond between
individual human feelings and age-old local traditions."
—*Famiglia Cristiana*
192 pp • $15.00 • 978-1-933372-83-9 • Territories: World

Milena Agus
From the Land of the Moon
"A jewel of a novel, it shines like a precious, exquisite gemstone."—
Libération
120 pp • $15.00 • 978-1-60945-001-4 • Territories: World except Australia & NZ

Salwa Al Neimi
The Proof of the Honey
"Al Neimi announces the end of a taboo in the Arab world: that of
sex!"—*Reuters*
144 pp • $15.00 • 978-1-933372-68-6 • Territories: World except UK

Alberto Angela
A Day in the Life of Ancient Rome
"Fascinating and accessible."—*Il Giornale*
392 pp • $16.00 • 978-1-933372-71-6 • Territories: World

Jenn Ashworth
A Kind of Intimacy
"Evokes a damaged mind with the empathy and confidence of Ruth Rendell."—*The Times*
416 pp • $15.00 • 978-1-933372-86-0 • Territories: USA & Canada

Beryl Bainbridge
The Girl in the Polka Dot Dress
"Very gripping, very funny and deeply mysterious."
—*The Spectator*
176 pp • $15.00 • 978-1-60945-056-4 • Territories: USA

Muriel Barbery
The Elegance of the Hedgehog
"Gently satirical, exceptionally winning and inevitably bittersweet."—*The Washington Post*
336 pp • $15.00 • 978-1-933372-60-0 • Territories: World except UK & EU

Gourmet Rhapsody
"In the pages of this book, Barbery shows off her finest gift: lightness."—*La Repubblica*
176 pp • $15.00 • 978-1-933372-95-2 • Territories: World except UK & EU

Stefano Benni
Margherita Dolce Vita
"A modern fable…hilarious social commentary."—*People*
240 pp • $14.95 • 978-1-933372-20-4 • Territories: World

Timeskipper
"Benni again unveils his Italian brand of magical realism."
—*Library Journal*
400 pp • $16.95 • 978-1-933372-44-0 • Territories: World

Romano Bilenchi
The Chill
"Accomplishes what books three times its length seek to do."
—*Boston Pheonix*
120 pp • $15.00 • 978-1-933372-90-7 • Territories: World

Kazimierz Brandys
Rondo
"[Brandy's has] quickened the conscience and enriched
the writing of the twentieth century."—*Time*
400 pp • $16.00 • 978-1-60945-004-5 • Territories: World

Alina Bronsky
Broken Glass Park
"Bronsky writes with a gritty authenticity and unputdownable
propulsion."—*Vogue*
336 pp • $15.00 • 978-1-933372-96-9 • Territories: World

The Hottest Dishes of the Tartar Cuisine
"Utterly entertaining. Rosa is an unreliable narrator par
excellence."—*FAZ*
304 pp • $15.00 • 978-1-60945-006-9 • Territories: World

Massimo Carlotto
The Goodbye Kiss
"A masterpiece of Italian noir."—*Globe and Mail*
160 pp • $14.95 • 978-1-933372-05-1 • Territories: World

Death's Dark Abyss
"A remarkable study of corruption and redemption."
—*Kirkus* (starred review)
160 pp • $14.95 • 978-1-933372-18-1 • Territories: World

The Fugitive
"[Carlotto is] the reigning king of Mediterranean noir."
—*The Boston Phoenix*
176 pp • $14.95 • 978-1-933372-25-9 • Territories: World

Bandit Love
"*Bandit Love* is a gripping novel that can be read on different
levels." —*Il Manifesto*
208 pp • $15.00 • 978-1-933372-80-8 • Territories: World

(with **Marco Videtta**)
Poisonville
"The business world as described by Carlotto and Videtta
in *Poisonville* is frightening as hell."
—*La Repubblica*
224 pp • $15.00 • 978-1-933372-91-4 • Territories: World

Francisco Coloane
Tierra del Fuego
"Coloane is the Jack London of our times."—*Alvaro Mutis*
192 pp • $14.95 • 978-1-933372-63-1 • Territories: World

Rebecca Connell
The Art of Losing
"This confident debut is both a thriller and an emotional portrait of
the long-term repercussions of infidelity."
—*Financial Times*
240 pp • $15.00 • 978-1-933372-78-5 • Territories: USA

Laurence Cossé
A Novel Bookstore
"An Agatha Christie-style mystery bolstered by a love story worthy of Madame de la Fayette . . ."—*Madame Figaro*
424 pp • $15.00 • 978-1-933372-82-2 • Territories: World

An Accident in August
"Cossé is a master of fine storytelling."—*La Repubblica*
208 pp • $15.00 • 978-1-60945-049-6 • Territories: World but not UK

Giancarlo De Cataldo
The Father and the Foreigner
"A slim but touching noir novel from one of Italy's best writers in the genre."—*Quaderni Noir*
144 pp • $15.00 • 978-1-933372-72-3 • Territories: World

Shashi Deshpande
The Dark Holds No Terrors
"[Deshpande is] an extremely talented storyteller."
—*Hindustan Times*
272 pp • $15.00 • 978-1-933372-67-9 • Territories: USA

Helmut Dubiel
Deep in the Brain: Living with Parkinson's Disease
"A book that begs reflection."—*Die Zeit*
144 pp • $15.00 • 978-1-933372-70-9 • Territories: World

Steve Erickson
Zeroville
"A funny, disturbing, daring and demanding novel—Erickson's best."—*The New York Times Book Review*
352 pp • $14.95 • 978-1-933372-39-6 • Territories: USA & Canada

Caryl Férey
Zulu
"Powerful and unflinching in its portrayal of evil both mindless and calculating."—*Publishers Weekly*
416 pp • $15.00 • 978-1-933372-88-4 • Territories: World except UK & EU

Elena Ferrante
The Days of Abandonment
"The raging, torrential voice of [this] author is something rare."—*The New York Times*
192 pp • $14.95 • 978-1-933372-00-6 • Territories: World

Troubling Love
"Ferrante's polished language belies the rawness of her imagery."—*The New Yorker*
144 pp • $14.95 • 978-1-933372-16-7 • Territories: World

The Lost Daughter
"So refined, almost translucent."—*The Boston Globe*
144 pp • $14.95 • 978-1-933372-42-6 • Territories: World

Linda Ferri
Cecilia
"A passionate and meticulous account of a young woman's search for her spiritual identity."—*La Repubblica*
288 pp • $15.00 • 978-1-933372-87-7 • Territories: World

Damon Galgut
In a Strange Room
"A taut, mesmerizing novel."—*New York Times*
224 pp • $15.00 • 978-1-60945-011-3 • Territories: USA

Jane Gardam
Old Filth
"Old Filth belongs in the Dickensian pantheon of memorable characters."—*The New York Times Book Review*
304 pp • $14.95 • 978-1-933372-13-6 • Territories: USA & Italy

The Queen of the Tambourine
"A truly superb and moving novel."—*The Boston Globe*
272 pp • $14.95 • 978-1-933372-36-5 • Territories: USA

The People on Privilege Hill
"Engrossing stories of hilarity and heartbreak."
—*Seattle Times*
208 pp • $15.95 • 978-1-933372-56-3 • Territories: USA

The Man in the Wooden Hat
"Here is a writer who delivers the world we live in…with memorable and moving skill."—*The Boston Globe*
240 pp • $15.00 • 978-1-933372-89-1 • Territories: USA

God on the Rocks
"A meticulously observed modern classic."
—*The Independent*
224 pp • $15.00 • 978-1-933372-76-1 • Territories: USA & Canada

Anna Gavalda
French Leave
"A comedy of happiness that will delight readers."
—*La Croix*
144 pp • $15.00 • 978-1-60945-005-2 • Territories: USA & Canada

Alicia Giménez-Bartlett
Dog Day
"Delicado and Garzón prove to be one of the more engaging sleuth teams to debut in a long time."—*The Washington Post*
320 pp • $14.95 • 978-1-933372-14-3 • Territories: USA & Canada

Prime Time Suspect
"A gripping police procedural."
—*The Washington Post*
320 pp • $14.95 • 978-1-933372-31-0 • Territories: USA & Canada

Death Rites
"Petra is developing into a good cop, and her earnest efforts to assert her authority...are worth cheering."—*The New York Times*
304 pp • $16.95 • 978-1-933372-54-9 • Territories: USA & Canada

Katharina Hacker
The Have-Nots
"Hacker's prose soars."—*Publishers Weekly*
352 pp • $14.95 • 978-1-933372-41-9 • World except India

Patrick Hamilton
Hangover Square
"Patrick Hamilton's novels are dark tunnels of misery, loneliness, deceit, and sexual obsession."
—*New York Review of Books*
336 pp • $14.95 • 978-1-933372-06-8 • Territories: USA & Canada

James Hamilton-Paterson
Cooking with Fernet Branca
"Irresistible!"—*The Washington Post*
288 pp • $14.95 • 978-1-933372-01-3 • Territories: USA

Amazing Disgrace
"It's loads of fun, light and dazzling as a peacock feather."
—*New York Magazine*
352 pp • $14.95 • 978-1-933372-19-8 • Territories: USA

Rancid Pansies
"Campy comic saga about hack writer and self-styled 'culinary
genius' Gerald Samper."—*Seattle Times*
288 pp • $15.95 • 978-1-933372-62-4 • Territories: USA

Seven-Tenths: The Sea and Its Thresholds
"The kind of book that, were he alive now, Shelley might have
written."—*Charles Spawson*
416 pp • $16.00 • 978-1-933372-69-3 • Territories: USA

Alfred Hayes
The Girl on the Via Flaminia
"Immensely readable."—*The New York Times*
164 pp • $14.95 • 978-1-933372-24-2 • Territories: World

Jean-Claude Izzo
Total Chaos
"Izzo's Marseilles is ravishing."—*Globe and Mail*
256 pp • $14.95 • 978-1-933372-04-4 • Territories: USA & Canada

Chourmo
"A bitter, sad and tender salute to a place equally impossible to love
or leave."—*Kirkus* (starred review)
256 pp • $14.95 • 978-1-933372-17-4 • Territories: USA & Canada

Solea
"[Izzo is] a talented writer who draws from the deep, dark well of noir."—*The Washington Post*
208 pp • $14.95 • 978-1-933372-30-3 • Territories: USA & Canada

The Lost Sailors
"Izzo digs deep into what makes men weep."
—*Time Out New York*
272 pp • $14.95 • 978-1-933372-35-8 • Territories: World

A Sun for the Dying
"Beautiful, like a black sun, tragic and desperate."
—*Le Point*
224 pp • $15.00 • 978-1-933372-59-4 • Territories: World

Gail Jones
Sorry
"Jones's gift for conjuring place and mood rarely falters."
—*Times Literary Supplement*
240 pp • $15.95 • 978-1-933372-55-6 • Territories: USA & Canada

Matthew F. Jones
Boot Tracks
"A gritty action tale."—*The Philadelphia Inquirer*
208 pp • $14.95 • 978-1-933372-11-2 • Territories: USA & Canada

Ioanna Karystiani
The Jasmine Isle
"A modern Greek tragedy about love foredoomed and family life."—*Kirkus*
288 pp • $14.95 • 978-1-933372-10-5 • Territories: World

Swell
"Karystiani movingly pays homage to the sea and those who live from it."—*La Repubblica*
256 pp • $15.00 • 978-1-933372-98-3 • Territories: World

Gene Kerrigan
The Midnight Choir
"The lethal precision of his closing punches leave quite a lasting mark."—*Entertainment Weekly*
368 pp • $14.95 • 978-1-933372-26-6 • Territories: USA & Canada

Little Criminals
"A great story…relentless and brilliant."
—*Roddy Doyle*
352 pp • $16.95 • 978-1-933372-43-3 • Territories: USA & Canada

Peter Kocan
Fresh Fields
"A stark, harrowing, yet deeply courageous work of immense power and magnitude."—*Quadrant*
304 pp • $14.95 • 978-1-933372-29-7 • Territories: USA, Canada and Europe

The Treatment and the Cure
"Kocan tells this story with grace and humor."
—*Publishers Weekly*
256 pp • $15.95 • 978-1-933372-45-7 • Territories: USA, Canada and Europe

Helmut Krausser
Eros
"Helmut Krausser has succeeded in writing a great German epochal novel."—*Focus*
352 pp • $16.95 • 978-1-933372-58-7 • Territories:World

Amara Lakhous
Clash of Civilizations Over an Elevator in Piazza Vittorio
"Do we have an Italian Camus on our hands?
Just possibly."—*The Philadelphia Inquirer*
144 pp • $14.95 • 978-1-933372-61-7 • Territories: World

Lia Levi
The Jewish Husband
"Levi's crystalline prose gradually generates an emotional
groundswell of unexpected intensity."—*Publishers Weekly*
224 pp • $15.00 • 978-1-933372-93-8 • Territories: World

Carlo Lucarelli
Carte Blanche
"Lucarelli proves that the dark and sinister are better evoked when
one opts for unadulterated grit and grime."
—*The San Diego Union-Tribune*
128 pp • $14.95 • 978-1-933372-15-0 • Territories: World

The Damned Season
"De Luca…is a man both pursuing and pursued. And that makes
him one of the more interesting figures in crime fiction."—*The
Philadelphia Inquirer*
128 pp • $14.95 • 978-1-933372-27-3 • Territories: World

Via delle Oche
"Delivers a resolution true to the series'
moral relativism." —*Publishers Weekly*
160 pp • $14.95 • 978-1-933372-53-2 • Territories: World